MONICA

Saunders Lewis

Translated by Meic Stephens

Afterword by Bruce Griffiths

seren

seren is the book imprint of
Poetry Wales Press Ltd,
Wyndham Street, Bridgend,
CF31 1EF, Wales

ISBN: 1-85411-195-7

A CIP record for this title is available from
the British Library

*The publisher acknowledges the financial support
of the Arts Council of Wales*

Cover illustration: 'Lady in a black hat (portrait of Mrs Erna Meinel)'
by Evan Walters reproduced by permission of The Glynn Vivian Art
Gallery, The City and County of Swansea

Printed in Plantin by Creative Print and Design, Ebbw Vale

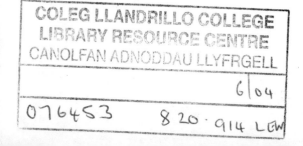

Chapter One

'Just listen to that woman again.'

'The one who's laughing?'

'She never stops. It's getting on my nerves. Every evening she and her husband are out there chatting with Mrs North, and never mind what the husband says, she finds it funny, and goes into peals of laughter. Haven't you seen her? Go over to the window.'

The younger of the two sisters came round the bed and looked out at the newly-built houses across the road. She saw the laughing woman's back, her hand resting on the handle of a lawn-mower, and her husband standing near by. Their heads were tilted upwards, because Mrs North was leaning out of a window above them and a little to the left. The new houses were semi-detached; each pair, neat and compact, would have made a fair-sized house.

'Is that her with the curly blonde shingled hair?'

'Yes, and that's her husband. You can't see her face yet. She's pretty, but she has the face of a spoilt child, and a snub nose. Her name's MacEwan, according to Mrs North, and they've been married three years. There, she's turning round now.'

'She's an odd shape.'

'She's expecting a child. Look, there are the cats coming out

5

through the door. They were in the garden all morning. They're hers, I'd wager.'

'Now, Alice, you must lie down and try to sleep.'

'Don't close the curtains, will you? It's so light now that the clocks have gone forward, and the moon will be up before the sun goes down. I'll be able to look out of the window if I can't sleep, and then I shan't notice the hours passing.'

Her sister left her. Alice sat up again and peered out at the people across the road. It was after nine o'clock on a fine evening in late April. A full moon had come up and it was so light outside that it could still have been day. Alice saw Mrs MacEwan's golden hair flap like wings about her head as she laughed, and her green silk dress hung loosely about her hips. Presently Mrs North closed her window and the couple began moving around the garden. Mrs MacEwan called to her two white cats and, still laughing, coaxed them to her. One lay on the lawn, rolling over and over provocatively in the moonlight. The tom sat and watched her. Suddenly he pounced on her.

The she-cat let out a long, plaintive miaow, and Mrs Mac-Ewan laughed. Alice felt her stomach turn. She slumped back down on the bed. She felt sick.

Lily ran in.

'You shouldn't try to sit up, with your weak heart. You know that full well.'

'I'll be all right in a minute.'

'Whatever came over you?'

'I don't know. I don't know. It's passed now.'

She lay back, pale and upset.

'You can go now.'

Next day, while Lily was in the garden, Alice saw Mrs North and Mrs MacEwan crossing the road towards her house. She saw the usual formalities, the how-d'you-dos, the smiles, the animated talk, a good deal of earnest explanation, and an obvious request that made Lily pause and think for a moment.

Alice could see that something interesting was about to happen. She saw a shy, imploring look on Mrs MacEwan's face, and some hesitation on her sister's. Presently Lily came into the house, leaving the two neighbours in the garden.

'What do you think? Can Mrs MacEwan come to sleep here tonight?'

Alice looked excited. Her sister misunderstood her expression.

'If you're not willing, she doesn't have to. I can say you're not well enough.'

'I'm all right. Of course she can. But why?'

'Mr MacEwan is away on business and she's afraid of being in the house on her own. Mrs North can't put her up. I offered to let one of the maids go over to stay with her, but she said that wouldn't be convenient, either.'

'The bedroom's ready. Now we've got neighbours, we'll have to be civil to them.'

'That's what I thought. She can come over this afternoon while I'm out.'

'Yes, let her come early. I'm quite better today.'

Why did I get so excited? wondered Alice. Was it because I wanted to see her, common as she is? She watched Mrs MacEwan running back happily to her own house. How well-kept was her house? Why didn't she want the maid to stay with her? Never since she had come to live in the new road had anyone called on her and nobody had spoken to her except her husband, Mrs North and the tradesmen on their rounds.

That afternoon Mrs MacEwan sat at her neighbour's bedside near the window. She had put on a loose black dress with a scarlet knot at the shoulder. But Alice noticed there was grime under her fingernails, and she didn't like the heady, sweet scent she had brought into the room. The visitor sat uncomfortably, as if she were glad to be there but unsure what impression she was making. Her thick, clumsy fingers were knitting something woollen, and she said, with a half-smile:

'I have to get clothes ready.'

'When are you expecting it?'

'In another four months.'

She put the wool on her lap and was quiet for a moment. Then, turning abruptly to Alice:

'I detest the baby and I haven't even seen it. I'm not going to live, you know.'

Mrs MacEwan laughed uncontrollably. Alice closed her eyes in pain. She disliked this uncouth woman, and yet, confronted with this sudden outburst, she was shamed into making a kind response. Slowly she opened her eyes:

'You shouldn't have such thoughts, Mrs MacEwan. You'll come through all right.'

'How old do you think I am?'

There was no evading her. Alice looked anxiously at her child-like nose and chin, and at the pencil-lines rather too heavily drawn on her eyebrows and lips. She could make out nothing to suggest her age save for a few crows' feet around the eyes. She's three years younger than I am, thought Alice, and said:

'Thirty-two?'

Mrs MacEwan gave a sly, self-satisfied laugh:

'That's what my husband thinks, too, but I'm thirty-eight.'

Alice felt the conversation was a snare. She began to be afraid of this woman, afraid of what she might say next. Her bad manners were so blunt and invasive, her way of speaking so like removing a dressing from a wound, to reveal the horrid, stark and stinking pus underneath it. I have to get myself out of this, thought Alice, but in her fright she misjudged it and only slipped deeper into the trap:

8

'What does Mr MacEwan do?'

'Jewellery and clock business. Usually he helps in the shop, but sometimes he travels around. He works mostly for the ships, repairing clocks and compasses. Whenever a ship comes into harbour the captain always prefers to have the same craftsman reset the compasses, if he's not too far away. That's why he's gone to Cardiff today. But business hasn't been at all good these last few months, and I hate having to skimp all the time and do the housework myself. Actually, I don't. I leave it until Bob comes home. He does it all for me.'

'Really, you do have a considerate husband.'

Alice breathed more easily. She felt the danger recede as the conversation took a more ordinary and prosaic turn:

'It's no credit to him. He does it all out of self-interest, so that I can look pretty and cheerful for him, make a pet of him, cuddle and embrace him. He can't do without that. That's why it's so easy to punish him.'

Alice looked out through the window and saw the two cats on the lawn of the house across the way. One began to play and frolic, but the other was not in the mood and slowly got up and slunk out of sight. Its companion grovelled after it.

'Did you put the cats out?'

'Yes, the pretty little things. I've left plenty of milk for them in a dish in the backyard. What will become of them, I wonder?'

'How do you mean?'

'When I'm dead. They at least will miss me. I shall see to that.'

'Why do you have to imagine yourself dying? Think about living, the baby you're going to have, looking after it and bringing it up. That's the way to dispel your fears.'

'I am not afraid, Miss Evans.'

'Is there no one to take care of you? A relative?'

Mrs MacEwan laughed bitterly:

'My father and sister, for instance? Neither of them will come here until I'm laid out for burial.'

Suddenly the floodgates opened. Monica MacEwan saw the chance for which she had been longing, a chance to pour out her memories, to explain all that had happened and, in particular, to justify herself. Up to now, there had never been anyone who understood her, or who would not have despised her had they heard her secret. She had somehow sensed that this bedridden woman was not one such but one of the few who, being of too courteous, too refined a nature, would not condemn anyone. She seized her opportunity. Out of her heart there poured an account of experiences and excuses that was a mixture of the true and the false. She spoke hurriedly as if she would never have another opportunity of defending herself. Alice, as she listened, thought it was an old story, one that she had rehearsed a hundred times in her loneliness. Indeed, before it was over she was virtually talking to herself. She almost forgot about Alice, who was able to lie back on her pillow, close her eyes and see it all just as Mrs MacEwan described it.

The rather shabby shop in Cardiff, the living quarters above it, and the mother wasting away with consumption. Invalids are not the only victims of ill health. It can sometimes ravage the strength of youth, snatching it from the joys of life and shackling it to a bedside where it has to wait, amid the fug and stench, on death's victim. If there is no relief, it comes to bear the mark of futility, of separation from joy. Monica spent the years of her youth like a bird beating against the bars of a cage. The clink of medicine bottles measured the hours for her, and the focus of her life moved from the bed's shadow to the wan light of the sofa by the window where her mother lay whenever the sun was shining. For a few years Monica had helped occasionally in the shop, but after her sister, ten years younger, had left school and was put to serve at the counter with her father, it fell to her to look after the upstairs, to do the housework, make the meals and tend the ailing mother. She saw little of her father. After closing his own premises, he would go to the workshop of an illiterate Jew who sold second-hand furniture. He kept his accounts and sent out bills on his behalf. By this means he supplemented the shop's scant takings in order to pay doctors and buy little luxuries of food and drink for his wife. Their younger daughter was her parents' favourite. After spending the day at the counter, she had to have some fresh air, they said, or else her strength would be sapped, and they could not afford to pay for help in the shop. So when of an evening she came into her mother's room, dressed all in white after a game of tennis, the sick woman's eyes would light up. She would whisper, 'Hannah is like the sun to me'. Monica's jealousy grew into hatred, and she rarely spoke to her sister. Two or three evenings a week Hannah took her place in the bedroom, and when Monica came home, she would be greeted with words that were like poison to her:

'You have a fine life, looking after Mother like this.'

There had been some things in Monica's background that she could not explain to anyone, not even to this bedridden woman who was trying to fill the emptiness of her own life by showing sympathy for the troubles of others. Even to her she could only hint at the thrills she had experienced twenty years before whenever she had stepped over the shop's threshold, closed the door and looked forward to three exhilarating hours out in the city's streets. She had preferred the dark months of winter to summer. In summer, horizons were broader and the half-empty streets at evening seemed sad, forgotten ways. The city was then merely part of a wider scene that stretched away in every direction, scattering people's souls in confusion to its furthermost limits. But on a winter's evening the heavens were lowered, so that no one looked up into the pitch black above the street-lamps. The horizons, too, were pressed towards each other, providing the city with warm, intimate boundaries. The eyes strayed neither up nor around, but the attention of the passers-by was fixed on one another, on the shops and on the bustle on all sides. In winter the country all around and the sky above were shut out in darkness, and the beams of life's light all focused as in a cinema on the enchanting film of Cardiff's streets.

Whenever she had money to spend, it was Monica's favourite treat to spend it in a tea-room. In summertime she would order ice-cream. At other times of year she would have Russian tea in a glass, a plate of French pastries, chocolate biscuits and macaroons. She sat long and blissfully as she tried each in turn, listening to the orchestra and watching the clientele moving about the tables. She was envious of the young women who passed by proudly and nonchalantly on the arms of their sweethearts. She noticed how an eager young man would proffer the menu to his companion, how she would peruse it in leisurely fashion, consult with him, and then order the meal without so much as raising her eyes to the waitress standing near by. Monica's heart was filled with admiration and envy. One evening, she thought, a young man would come in through the door, glance round the tables, until his eyes fell on her, and he would greet her, sit down beside her, and she, scarcely interrupting their conversation, would casually give an order to the waitress. Disturbed by the intensity of her day-dream, she raised her teacup to hide her face, lest anyone should notice her. More than once, indeed, some fellow or other tried surreptitiously to catch her eye from the café's entrance, and then Monica's heart would flutter with intense yearning, but she dared not look at him for fear she would cry aloud, and in an instant the opportunity would pass. Then, dejectedly, she too would get up and, after settling her bill, go out into the street.

'For years I had no companions and often longed for someone among the hundreds of people in the streets to speak to me.'

That is what Monica told Alice, attempting to conceal from her the seething cauldron of her memories. She had not wandered the streets haphazardly. Even now, in this room, the map of her excursions, every turning, every shop, every lamp on the way, was clear in her mind. There was a special ploy she used with lamps. On seeing a young man whom she fancied coming towards her, she would walk past him, cross the street behind him, and quickly turn back; having gained a hundred yards, she would cross the street and then turn again, thus contriving to come face to face with him once more, walking in the shadow under the lamp while all the light fell on the approaching man. In this way she could take a closer look at him without his being able to make her out clearly. Sometimes she was accosted; a voice would whisper, 'Good-evening' or 'Wait a moment, sweetie'. She would hurry past in anger. She was terrified of prostitutes and their clients. She knew the spots in the city where they congregated and she kept away from them. It never occurred to her that she was one of them. She was convinced that some day a young gentleman, one who had never picked up women in the street, would be destined to look at her and understand that she was not like other women, and break every rule by speaking to her. This time she would be ready and recognize the voice. That was why she went out walking the streets night after night. The nights turned into years and she did not give up hope. Sometimes her sister would happen to ask whether she might accompany her. No, Monica would say, I have a date. This could be the evening that Mr Right would appear. Her youth was swallowed up in expectation. Those whose lives are spent in perverse sexual fantasies often appear much younger than their years. On her twenty-sixth birthday Monica looked like a girl of twenty.

One evening she had gone out later than usual. Her mother had taken a turn for the worse; the doctor had been sent for and a poultice applied to the glands of her neck. Eventually, her mother said:

'You'd better go out for some fresh air. Hannah will see to me now.'

At this Monica hurried out. She made for the centre of the city. If her mother were to die, what would she do then? The idea came to her that evening for the very first time. Up to now, looking after the sick woman, squabbling with her and having to put up with her scolding, had been part of her life's pattern. Its unchanging routine had become indispensable to her, scaffolding for her fantasies. Without it, the fragile web of her dreams would have been torn asunder. It now occurred to her that, although she bore no love for her parents, to lose them would be a grievous blow, and she found herself, to her surprise, hoping that her mother would not die.

'Excuse me, isn't this your glove?'

A young man was straightening up from bending at her feet and he was offering her a glove. Monica had not seen him approach. She must have been flustered by her new thoughts, or she would never have been caught unawares like this. Her heart throbbed with the shock:

'Thank you,' she said hoarsely. 'I didn't know I'd dropped it.'

She put out her hand to receive the glove. She saw that she was already wearing gloves.

'But it's not mine. Look.'

Overcoming her confusion, she smiled. The young man smiled too:

'I thought sure I'd seen you dropping it. But I see now that it's not as pretty as yours. Please forgive me for troubling you.'

He raised his hat as if to take his leave of her. Monica, alarmed, said quickly:

'Whose is it, I wonder?'

The young man looked deep into her eyes:

'Out for a walk, are you? May I come with you?'

She nodded her assent and fell in at his side. They walked past the castle in the direction of Canton, her usual route. But now the pavement under her feet was like the waves of the sea.

'You're tired,' the young man said, misinterpreting her unsteadiness.

'Yes, I am. My mother's an invalid and I've been looking after her all day.'

'Let's go in here for an hour. There's quite a funny film on at the moment.'

He bought tickets. She followed the usher's torch until she was settled into one of the cinema's plush seats. In the darkness, with an unseen crowd all around her, she tried to regain her composure. She had not yet managed to steal a glance at her companion. Her dizzy feeling was still like a mist between them. All she knew was that he was short and stocky and smartly dressed, and that he spoke politely, an important attribute in her snobbish opinion. Even now in the kind half-light, she was unable to look at him, for she was aware that he was leaning back in his seat in order to look at her. But as he took a cigarette from its silver case and struck a match to light it, inclining his head to the flame, she glimpsed thick lips drawing on the cigarette, a heavy jaw, and a nose and forehead falling away like a half-ringlet from a flat crown. He might be twenty-one.

She felt it was high time to break the intense silence that had fallen between them. She whispered:

'Good picture, isn't it?'

He blew a puff of tobacco smoke into the warm darkness of the auditorium. He reached out and took hold of her arm. He placed two fingers on her wrist above the glove and felt her pulse. He could feel it racing. He let go and put his arm around her waist, pulling her to him. He asked:

'What's your name, my little mouse?'

'Monica Sheriff.'

'How old are you?'

'How old do you think?'

'Twenty?'

'Yes.'

'Give me a kiss.'

'No, not here. Everyone will see us.'

'No they won't, we're in the back row.'

'Don't, don't.'

He pressed her close. She turned her face to him and gave him one little peck on his moist lip. The next instant the lights of the auditorium came up. After they had gone down again, Monica whispered:

'Can I have that glove?'

'Yes. Here it is.'

'It was you who dropped it, wasn't it?'

'Of course it was.'

'To get to know me?'

'Exactly.'

'I shall keep this glove for as long as I live.'

The young man chuckled till the people sitting near by turned round to stare at them.

On leaving the cinema they walked up Cathedral Road towards Llandaff Fields. Monica walked in an ecstasy. She spoke little, her mind taken up with how she would introduce the young man to her parents and planning their future together. It was a night in October and the unlit road was unfamiliar to her. She did not mind in the least. The fantasies of years were at last becoming a reality.

'Let's sit here for a while,' said the young man, spreading his overcoat on the grass. Monica did as he asked, and went to sit at his side. He pulled her down until she was lying on the ground and the next instant she was frantically fighting him off. The effort became too much and she thought she was going to faint. She screamed with all the strength she had left.

The young man, releasing her, cursed:

'Do you want a policeman to catch us?'

'I didn't realize you were like that,' she said between her sobs.

'If that wasn't what you had in mind, why the hell did you come this way with me?'

'I thought we were sweethearts, that we were going to be married.'

Her companion guffawed long and loud. He got to his feet:

'Make yourself tidy.'

Monica did as she was told, her teeth chattering audibly.

'Stop your blubbing. I won't do anything to you, you silly girl. Come on now.'

He walked her to the tram terminus. He paid her fare and then left her. Monica said not a word, nor did she try to stop him paying. Her strength had completely deserted her. Only just before reaching home, she opened her silk handbag, took out a soiled white glove and threw it into an open drain in the gutter. Then she went into the house.

'Monica, are you going out?'

'No, Mother.'

'Hannah will see to me.'

'I'm not going out, Mother.'

Monica called to mind many such exchanges as she lied to Alice:

'For the last two years my mother was ill, I hardly went out at all.'

A few nights after the struggle in Llandaff she had tried to resume her old ways, but her step was not as brisk as before. To her great chagrin, she dared not go into a café, for if she came across him there, how would she escape? One evening she was loitering near James Howell's department store in St Mary's Street when she heard two people chatting loudly behind her. She recognized a voice saying:

'Just look at that hussy. She's walking the city's streets looking for a man to marry her. I tried to take pity on her —'

Monica did not wait to hear more. She ran as fast as her legs would carry her down Wharton Street, two coarse peals of laughter pursuing her like hounds. Thereafter she was in terror of the city. Whenever she had to go on an errand she would choose the back streets and the meanest shops.

The next two years were not entirely unhappy. Her mother's health deteriorated rapidly until she could no longer leave her bed. Her room became a place of refuge for her daughter. Neither told the other her most intimate thoughts, but at the last there grew between them a kind of unspoken understanding and sympathy. Her mother took no pleasure in watching Monica as she did when Hannah came to see her. But deep down inside she was vaguely aware that it was her illness which had caused, at least in part, the spiritual hurt that was afflicting her elder daughter, and so in her pity for Monica she found the same self-indulgent comfort as she felt in pitying herself. They spent an occasional happy half-hour in each other's company when Monica read her mother the day's instalment of a novel which was being serialized in the *Daily Mail*. At other times the daughter would sit at the window and describe the people she saw coming into and out of the shop. They had fun trying to guess what the customers wanted, and afterwards they would ask Hannah or her father to confirm whether they had been near the mark. Monica was a good nurse during these last months. She carried out her duties with steady, unflustered hands that soothed away the pain. Her mind preoccupied with other things, she never lost her head in a crisis but remained always unhurried and calm in her ministrations. Her mother was aware of this and never became upset.

Once, about three weeks before she died, Mrs Sheriff tried to persuade Monica to confide in her. She had seen her sitting at the window, the newspaper on her lap and the story having come to its conclusion with that day's episode. Monica had stopped reading and, after finishing the last sentence, peered for several minutes into the street below. Her mother called her to the bedside:

'Don't start the new story tomorrow.'

'All right, Mother.'

'I worry about you, my girl. Your father has the business, and Hannah will get married. She's young, she was made to be happy.'

'Can't I be happy, too?'

The mother shook her head for a long while. Then she said:

'You had some trouble with a young man about two years ago, didn't you?'

Monica went pale:

'How do you know?'

'I know. Tell me what's hurting you. I'm going to die soon. Your secret will be safe with me.'

'I've nothing to say.'

But she kissed her mother for the first time in years, and went to prepare tea. A month later the bed was empty and the medicine bottles, which had stood on the table for as long as she could remember, had disappeared from the room.

Chapter Two

'My mother's death didn't make all that difference to me,'
Monica told Alice. 'We went on much the same as before, my
father and Hannah in the shop, me about the house. The
business was looking up.'

She had continued to wear black for a year longer than her
sister. Thus she found the confidence to go out alone into the
streets again. She used to think mourning clothes were like a
concealing veil about her. She no longer employed the stratagems
of her adolescence. All that remained of her old habits was her
curiosity. She grew skilful at recognizing weak characters. She
observed the quiet men, of gentlemanly conduct, who con-
cealed their carnality under a cloak of shyness. She imagined
ways of exposing them. Then she was shocked by her own
thoughts and cast them aside. She slept uneasily at night.

The family usually had tea at six o'clock. One Wednesday,
early closing day, at about four in the afternoon, Monica came
in from visiting one of her old school friends. She climbed the
stairs in leisurely fashion and opened the parlour door. She
stopped and stood stock-still. Afternoon tea was laid out on a
small table by the fire, and her father and sister were sitting at
it with a young stranger. The three were laughing and had their
backs to her; they did not stir when she opened the door. Could
she escape the way she had come? Even as the thought flashed

through her mind, she had already in her surprise shut the door behind her. The stranger got to his feet.

'Monica,' said Hannah, 'this is Bob MacEwan, the man I'm going to marry.'

Somehow, she managed to offer him her hand.

'Sit here,' said her father, motioning her to a chair.

It was an afternoon in Autumn and daylight was already retreating gently from the hearth to a small strip near the window. Monica poured herself a cup of tea. She summoned up all her will-power to pour it precisely without spilling a drop. She had not taken in her sister's words. It was enough for the moment to try to grasp the fact that she was sitting in her own parlour face to face with a complete stranger. No young man had ever been there before. She had been used to seeing such a one as this in the street, in a café, outside, but not in here. To come across one in her own home laughing with her father was as if the enemy had caught a sentry unawares and unarmed inside a fortress. Monica nibbled at a crumb of cake. Although her throat was dry with shock, she dared not raise her cup to her lips.

Her father made an effort to carry on the conversation in the same tone as before, but just as a pebble that is thrown into a lake sends its ripples across the whole water, so Monica's trembling silence spread throughout the room.

Hannah leapt from her chair:

'Give me a match, Bob, I'll light up.'

'No, don't light up.'

Monica felt as if she had screeched her response, but Hannah had not heard. She lit the lamp. She tugged a cord at the corner of the window until the venetian blind came down with a thud. Monica looked at her sister's shapely back, her broad shoulders, and the athletic way she held herself. Hannah sat down at the piano and began to play a popular foxtrot. She handled the piano as gently as if it were a barrel-organ, calling out:

'Bob, come here and turn the pages for me. Light up your pipe, Daddy.'

With this command Hannah refocused the life of the room on herself, and her metallic music shut her sister out completely.

Suddenly Monica was afraid of her. Surprised, she thought: Of course, she's of an age to marry. She did not dare look at the young man who was bending over the piano adoringly.

At last Mr Sheriff tapped his pipe on the mantelpiece:

'I have to go and see my Jew.'

'We'll see you off,' replied Hannah. And within three minutes of moving chairs and donning hats and coats and saying their good-byes, Monica stood alone in the middle of the room. She stood quite still, with vacant eyes, her mind groping back to take in all that had happened since the moment she had opened the door. Like one who has been asleep for a short while and dreaming, but now in the shock of awakening is unable to recall the dream, she tried in vain to grasp those twenty minutes. Although she shut her eyes tightly she could see nothing save the image of her sister, — the other person was completely in her shadow. There was a knock on the door. Monica opened her eyes and saw Bob MacEwan standing there.

'I beg your pardon, Hannah's left her fur behind. Have you seen it?'

'There it is, on the chair.'

He snatched up the fur so quickly that it might have been a rabbit about to escape, and then he stroked it with his fingertips as if fondling it. He smiled oddly at Monica:

'Women's clothes are such nice things.'

Before she could reply, he added:

'I never had a sister. Having a sister will be as strange for me as having a wife.'

Suddenly he laughed:

'May I begin now by calling you Monica?'

'You may, I suppose, — Bob.'

He laughed again:

'Thank you. I'd better rush now after Hannah. Good-night, Monica. You have a pretty name.'

'God knows, I never did anything to entice him away from Hannah,' Monica said earnestly to Alice in the quiet of the bedroom. 'I hadn't known he existed before opening the door that afternoon. Neither my father nor my sister had told me about him. I was treated like a maid about the house. Bob told me that Hannah had never breathed a word to him about me. He hadn't liked to question her. Neither before he saw me nor afterwards was my name ever on her lips. And yet he maintains it was in that moment he came back to fetch the fur that he lost his heart to me. I was so calm and entrancing, he says.'

It was true that she had been calm, so very calm that her smile, which had spread across her face at the young man's words, did not falter but remained there for long after he had gone. She stood motionless, except that her lips slowly pursed.

No, she was not guilty of scheming to betray her sister, not at that moment, anyway. No firm intention or idea had come into her mind at all. But in her mind's eye there was an image of Bob MacEwan holding the fur, closing the door, going down the stairs, past the shop to the house's private door, out into the street, and then spreading the fur and proudly, solicitously draping it around the shoulders of the woman who was waiting for him. But when Monica looked at the woman's face, she saw that it was not Hannah but herself.

In Hannah's presence Bob MacEwan never looked at Monica. He spoke to her politely as to a stranger. That gladdened her heart. She learnt where his weakness lay and in her sister's hearing she was forgiving. But if occasionally he was deep in conversation with her father, she had only to pass by his chair and let the cuff of her sleeve, as if by accident, touch the nape of his neck and her perfume waft into his nostrils, to observe how it agitated him. She was content. She took care not to remain alone with him in a room.

Thus, without any word of intimacy, there grew between them a kind of secret understanding. Her hidden wantonness was revealed to him. She discovered his vulnerability. They came to depend on each other; he said nothing that would compromise her, and she left him quite alone with Hannah. The tension between them disappeared. The others felt the effect of it and Monica's father and sister drew closer to her.

'Whatever's come over you?' Mr Sheriff asked her one morning towards the end of November. 'You look like a young girl again.'

Christmas was drawing near. Every evening Bob MacEwan came to the house and he and Hannah put up holly and mistletoe and paper lanterns in an attempt to dispel its dreariness and gloom. Despite her father's misgivings, Hannah took on a girl to work in the shop over the festive season, added substantially to the usual stock of luxury goods, decorated the window, and turned her initiative into profit. Her father said:

'You're going to leave me just when you've got the business in hand. This is the first Christmas we've shown a profit.'

Mr Sheriff bought a bottle of port wine for Christmas lunch and Bob MacEwan was invited.

'I think,' said the father at table, 'that you and Bob shouldn't wait two years until you can afford a house. You ought to get married in the Spring and come here to live. You, Hannah, can go on helping in the shop and Monica can have a maid to help her. It'll be a fair deal.'

There was a toast to future success and the lovers' eyes sparkled as they raised their glasses. After lunch, Monica could no longer bear the glow on their faces. She went to her room that was on the same floor as the parlour.

'I'm going to lie down,' she said.

She took off her clothes and put on her dressing-gown of pink silk and swansdown. She stood before the mirror gazing at her reflection. The wine had brought out bright red flushes on the skin of her forehead and cheeks. She could see that her mouth was half-open and the tip of her tongue resting on her lip as if she were thirsty. But she did not try to compose her face, as she was wont to do. Instead, she listened. She heard the parlour door being opened and the couple laughing and whispering at the top of the stairs.

'Hurry up,' whispered Hannah, under the mistletoe, and Monica listened intently to the sound of kissing. She scarcely noticed that her own lips were pursed as she did so. Hannah ran up the next flight of stairs to her room, calling: 'Give me three minutes while I dress, wait there for me.' At this Monica picked up a towel and sponge as if she were on her way to the bathroom. She opened her door and went out onto the landing. Bob MacEwan caught her under the mistletoe and pulled her to him, kissing her. Suddenly he felt two lips prising his apart and a tongue licking under his own. Then, shocked, he let go of her and she slipped back into her room. Not a word had passed between them.

'It was on Christmas afternoon, under the mistletoe, that we kissed each other for the first time,' Monica told Alice. 'It was done frivolously, as such things are at Christmas time. I can hardly believe that Bob had given it any previous thought. I don't think he was yet aware that he didn't love Hannah. It wasn't love that he felt for her, only pride because he had managed to catch her.'

'What were your sister's feelings?'

Mrs MacEwan shrugged her shoulders in bewilderment:

'I never could make out what was going on in Hannah's heart. She was like a bell as far as I was concerned, always giving out the same glad chime. It was only from Bob, later on, that I heard what became of her.'

But for one whole week thereafter Bob had not set foot in the house. He could be heard saying good-night to Hannah on the doorstep.

'Why doesn't he come in?' asked Mr Sheriff.

'How should I know?' answered Hannah. Then she discreetly added, believing that her sister could not hear:

'Our trouble is that Bob's sentimental and I'm not.'

Monica stifled a happy sigh. So, she thought, he's keeping his distance because he's afraid of being unfaithful to her, and she's upset because he's been trying to get her to kiss him like I did. When at last he did come to supper, on New Year's Eve, Monica stayed in her room on the pretext of having a headache. Her knees trembled when she heard his footstep on the landing.

Over the next fortnight she braced herself to face the inevitable. After all, this wonderful thing was about to happen to *her*. Sometimes she gazed for minutes on end at a picture of her mother, smiling and murmuring: 'You'll see, you'll see'. On getting into bed she wondered, How many more times shall I lie here? The shadow of what was to come fell across everything she did, lending ardour to such daily chores as sweeping a room or folding sheets. She stared hard around each bedroom as she tidied it: I must remember where that corner cupboard was and this picture of me as a child. She withdrew into her expectation as into a cloak. In less than a week she had slipped back into the mental processes of her adolescence. Saying little, she grew more and more detached from her family. ('Sulking again, as usual,' commented Mr Sheriff.) She planned nothing. She had no idea how it might come about, but her mind was gripped and absorbed by the certainty that *afterwards* she and he would have to leave this house and turn their backs on her old life. It was her destiny, not her intention. Because of this patient streak in her nature, her ability to slither aimlessly on the slope of her sensuality, she had been able to convince herself that she was innocent in her behaviour towards her sister. It was not her fault that this was going to happen; it was in the nature of things. She nevertheless knew that the moment would come when she would have to take action and make herself the ready, proper and complete instrument of her own fate. The thrill of it made her tremble all over. She did not doubt her capacity nor her instinctive readiness for it. But it cost her dear, and her silence about the house turned into something alive and hostile, filling her sister and father also, though they did not understand the cause, with apprehension.

One morning Mr Sheriff went into the bathroom and Monica heard the snip of his scissors trimming his beard in front of the glass. He was in a hurry.

A moment later Hannah came down for her cold bath — she was the only one who took a daily cold bath all year round. Seeing the short bristles left on the rim of the basin, she ran to her father's door and hammered on it wildly:

'Father, your hair's made a mess of the basin. I can't wash in there. It's disgusting.'

Hannah had never been known to tell her father off. Monica suddenly felt shame and pity. She ran into the bathroom before her father could get there, turned on the tap and wiped the basin. When he arrived, Monica said:

'Never mind, I've washed it away. Don't take any notice of Hannah's bad temper. She's having trouble with Bob.'

Mr Sheriff looked stunned. Monica's tenderness was odder than Hannah's rage. As he went back to his room, he wondered to himself, What does she know about Bob?

Monica had been right. When Bob MacEwan had come to the house on New Year's Eve, a load had been lifted from his mind when she did not come in to supper. Reassured that he would not see her, he grew more relaxed and more like his usual self. His apprehension had gone and before leaving he promised to return next evening.

'Why don't you take that holly down now?' he asked on the landing. There was no holly, only mistletoe. The following night, Monica still not having appeared, he once again felt uncomfortable.

Now he yearned to see her, to exchange glances and talk discreetly and give the impression, as they habitually did, that all was well again. He would not be wholly at ease, nor safe, unless he saw her. Each time the door opened he would look up eagerly and anxiously, but it was only Hannah or Mr Sheriff.

Why didn't she come? His need to see her had begun to take possession of him. To see her and start all over again on normal terms, only then would the poisonous memory of their kissing be eradicated. He found himself regretting that Hannah could not kiss like that.

The next day, Bob came to the house half an hour before the shop's closing time, and so had an excuse to wait in the parlour. He was there on his own for some twenty minutes. A meal had been set on the table. Twice Bob opened the door. He wondered whether she was down in the kitchen or close by in her bedroom. Once he almost went to knock on her door. He could hear no sound at all except for those coming from the shop. At last Hannah came in and began preparing the food. He stood near the fire, biting his nails and spitting the bits into the grate. As casually as he could manage, he asked:

'Where's your sister?'

'She went out through the back a quarter of an hour ago.'

Hannah was tired and upset because he had arrived before she had time to spruce herself up:

'Why did you come early? You know I'm not free before seven.'

'If I'm in the way, I can go . . . .'

'Just as you please.'

But Mr Sheriff came in and they sat down to table.

Hannah, these days, could not bear him to embrace her. Whenever they went out and he tried to take her arm she would shake herself free:

'What's the matter?'

'I prefer to walk on my own.'

When they kissed good-night, she would turn her cheek to him, but he could not let his lips linger on hers. One evening when they had been to the theatre together, she handed him her key as usual, so that he could open the front door for her; then, with her foot on the threshold, she said:

'It was grand tonight, Bob. Don't let's spoil it all by kissing. Good-night.'

She closed the door behind her.

Bob MacEwan turned to go home. I must see Monica, he told himself over and over again. If only I can see her and talk to her for a few minutes, everything will be all right again. I can't bear this any longer. The look on Hannah's face at the door. My own sweetheart. Why is she afraid of kissing me? I can't stand seeing her worry. If I could see Monica and tell her there was nothing in it . . . I've got to see her . . . .'

He had one hand on the gate of his lodgings and the other was rummaging in his pocket for a key. But suddenly he shut the gate, buttoned up his coat and began striding hurriedly back. Every now and again he broke into a run. His mind was now made up. He had a clear mental picture of the house: the shop on the street, the parlour immediately above it, then Mr Sheriff's room over the house's private entrance, Hannah's room on the upper floor under the eaves. Only Monica slept at the back, on the first floor above the kitchen. There was a narrow lane between the high walls of the yards and it led to the house's back door; it was known as the entry. It was towards the entry that Bob MacEwan was now making, and as he ran he broke his stride at irregular intervals to bend down into the gutter, pick up a small stone and put it in his pocket. At last here was the street for which he had been making. There was no light in the parlour nor in Mr Sheriff's room, but under the eaves he could see a blue light behind Hannah's curtain and from time to time her shadow was cast on it. She was about to go to bed. Bob MacEwan counted the shops and houses to the end of the street, then turned right until he came to the entry and counted the back doors down to number fifteen. This was the house. In wild haste now, he glanced to left and right. There was no one about. He struck a match and looked at his watch. It was a quarter to midnight. He did up his coat and took a leap. His fingers found a hold in the wall above the yard door, he dragged himself up and the sole of his shoe came to rest on the latch. A moment later he was crouching on top of the wall.

There was a light in Monica's room. Bob looked about him and heard rain beginning to fall. The night was so dark that he could see no more in the yard than if it had been a deep pit. He reckoned there were twenty yards between him and the lit window. He sat on the wall, took a stone from his pocket and threw it gingerly at the pane. The stone fell onto a wooden box. He threw another. The second stone hit the kitchen window and fell noisily to the ground. Breathless, Bob paused expectantly. There was no response, no sound whatsoever. From where he was sitting he was unable to throw in safety, and he did not dare call out. There was only one thing for it. He tucked up the tails of his overcoat and, clutching them, leapt into the yard. As he fell he collided with the metal dustbin and the lid clattered loudly onto the flagstones. A dog next door started barking fiercely. He heard a door open and voices calling, and saw a lamp passing a window. Panic seized him. He fumbled for the latch of the backyard door. But it was barred and he could not find the bar. He heard Mr Sheriff shouting and someone letting out the dog next door, which then ran into the yard barking. Bob tried to jump back onto the wall, but lost his hold and fell. Before he could get up again, he felt a hand taking him by the arm. Monica pulled him towards the door, drew the bar and pushed him into the lane:

'Run to the right, there's a turning in the entry there.'

Without more ado the young man made his escape and, turning round, she looked into the light of her father's lamp.

Only as he was about to undress at nearly two o'clock that morning did Bob MacEwan notice that he was soaked to the skin.

'That Monday evening I knew things weren't right between them,' Monica said after finishing her cup of tea. 'I saw Hannah on the stairs after she had said good-night to Bob. She was in tears. She ran past me and slammed her door. She was in a temper because I'd caught her crying. Nor could I go to bed. Twice I went out onto the landing to listen. It was there I heard someone in the backyard. I can't say how I was so sure it was Bob. I went down into the kitchen and while I was there a stone struck the window. I was in two minds whether I should go out to him or not. A moment later the noise of his falling could be heard all over the house. My father got up. He shouted to me, asking whether it was me making the noise. I could hear him lighting the lamp and barely had a chance to run out to Bob and open the back door for him to make his escape.'

'It was quite natural after that for him to write to me. His letter came on Wednesday morning, a brief note asking me whether I'd meet him near the city library at mid-day. He said he wouldn't keep me more than five minutes but that it was important to him. I didn't go. I didn't think it was fair to Hannah. I knew now that we must meet only when she was present, and that I didn't have the right to see him behind her back. I couldn't have known then that, in fact, he was already a free man, and had written to me immediately after receiving a letter from her. Her letter had been delivered with the late post on Tuesday evening. I was shown it the following Sunday in Bob's lodgings, the only letter she'd ever written him. I've kept it ever since because it's proof that I'm not guilty as regards Hannah. Listen to it, you'll see at once how unsuitable she was for a man like Bob.'

Monica took the letter from her purse and read it aloud:

> Dear Bob,
>
> I can't come with you to the Vale tomorrow afternoon as I promised. The rep. will be calling on Thursday and I shall have to sacrifice my half-day off in order to check the stock.
>
> Perhaps this is not entirely a bad thing. Things haven't been too smooth between us these last few days, and I have my doubts whether I can be as good a partner for you in life as I am in a game of tennis. My feelings towards you are too genuine to allow me to deceive myself over such a matter. If that is what you fear too, I'm ready now to release you from every promise you've made. Think it over, and come here on Sunday afternoon, — not before. — H.
>
> P.S. Burglars tried to break in through the back last night.

'You'd be surprised, Miss Evans, how easily everything came to an end. Bob came to the house shortly after lunch that Sunday. I was almost dressed ready to go out. Of course, I had no idea he was coming, but I recall opening a new bottle of scent and I was spraying it on my hair and down my front when the bell rang. My father went to the door and I heard Bob asking for Hannah and saying, 'I must see her at once'. My father replied rather drily — it was his rest-hour — but he went up to tell Hannah. She was always a very slow one dressing. I had long since finished and eventually I went into the parlour.'

'He looked like death itself. "Aren't you well?" I asked. "I caught a cold on Tuesday night," he answered, "and had to stay in bed yesterday and the day before," and then he added, "I'm in serious trouble, Monica." He was swaying on his feet, and though he looked so ashen, beads of perspiration stood out on his forehead. I took my handkerchief and went up to him to wipe his brows. But in an instant, he grabbed me and kissed me, all the while crying, "Monica, Oh, Monica".'

'That was how Hannah saw us. I'd heard her on the stairs, but why should I have resisted him? She stared at us for a long time. I saw her go pale and her eyes growing wild and then lifeless. She walked out of the room and I heard her collapse on the landing. I couldn't go to her because Bob had slumped onto the sofa crying, "What shall I do, what shall I do, Monica?", and was clinging to my arm.'

'That Sunday, from the moment Bob turned to me like that, remains with me to this day, the only day of pure triumph I've had in my whole life. I could see he was about to faint and that he was dangerously feverish. There was nothing for it but to remove anything that might cause him distress. As gently as I could, I took from his finger the ring Hannah had given him. I undid his waistcoat so that he could breathe more easily. I sat down on the sofa and drew his head onto my breast. I heard my father taking Hannah up to his own room, so there was no need to see to her. I laid my fingers on his forehead and cheeks to cool them, and presently he revived. He pulled my face down to his. He was giving himself to me completely, like a wilful child that has suddenly become amenable and ready to do as it's told. "You must speak to them, Monica," he said. "I can't do any more." I whispered to him, "Don't worry, you're mine now. Leave everything to me".'

'I went into my bedroom to get dressed. I put a few things into my bag and hurriedly washed myself and did my hair. Then I knocked on my father's door. "I'm taking Bob back to his lodgings," I said. My father answered quietly and courteously enough, "Yes, that would be best." He closed his door and I called to Bob. We found a taxi at the end of the street and very soon we were at his lodgings. Mrs Nesbit opened the door and wasn't at all surprised to see us. "I told him, Miss Sheriff," she said, "he didn't ought to have gone out, but he insisted on it, saying it was very important business." She was a comical old lady and I couldn't help smiling as she went on: "So you're Miss Sheriff. You aren't at all like your picture, you're older but much more pleasant. The night before last, you know, he was maundering a bit in his delirium, and calling your full name — Hannah Monica".'

'Bob went to bed straightaway and Mrs Nesbit lit a fire for us in his room and we had tea together. I re-arranged the room and tidied everything up, — you know what a bachelor's bedroom is like. I felt like a monarch who had acquired a new kingdom, and I went down and tidied his parlour too; it was at the back of the house. I saw two pictures of Hannah there and a few other things that had come from her. I had to burn them. And I altered the arrangement of the table and chairs and Mrs Nesbit gave me flowers and fresh curtains. What I wanted most of all was to create a completely new atmosphere around Bob so that he would feel himself in a different world — my world. It was as I was going through a drawer to tidy some papers that I came across Hannah's letter.'

'By that evening Bob was better. He was singing and embracing me and fooling about. "You're as deep and bewitching as a cat," he said, laughing and kissing me. "I did my best not to lose my head over you, but it wasn't any use." My only response was to kiss him again as I'd done the first time. We were married a month later, at the registry office in Cardiff. My father gave me a cheque for two hundred pounds the night before I left home, and said: "I don't want to see you ever again." He and Hannah were serving at the counter as I went out through the shop next morning to the taxi; I bade them good-bye but neither said a word to me. We left Cardiff two years later and came to live here in Swansea. I haven't heard from them since.'

'But you still have your husband,' said Alice.

Mrs MacEwan turned on her sharply:

'Do you think, Miss Evans, that love brings happiness? The whole point of love is this,' she said, indicating her pregnancy. 'It's for this that two people crave each other and kiss each other, and for all their hatred, can't leave each other alone. I'm as jealous of my husband today as I was when he was engaged to Hannah. If someone else tried to have him, I'd use every trick I know to get my own back on both of them. And yet I can't stand my husband.'

Chapter Three

'Good-morning to you now.'

From their window the two sisters watched their neighbour crossing the road back to her own house. She walked un-hurriedly. She knew that they were watching her, but did not once turn round.

'She's like someone on her way to be hanged,' said Lily. 'Look, the cats have come to meet her at the gate. Why's she standing there so long?'

Monica had flung open the door and was waiting for the cats to go in first. The morning sun was shining from the south-east and her shadow was cast before her into the porch. Suddenly she turned to face the sun and raised her hand to wave to the sisters. She seemed to be bidding the sun good-bye. Then she stepped into her own shadow and, closing the door firmly, shut out the light. A shiver ran through Alice.

Monica closed the door and went upstairs to her bedroom intending to change. She opened the window. Her cigarette-case was near the mirror on the dressing-table. She took out a cigarette, lit it and sat down on the feather bed to smoke. It was ten o'clock. In half an hour the milk-boy would be calling. Then the grocer's cart would come round and the fishmonger's after that. Thus she would get the provisions necessary to make herself a meal at mid-day. She ought to go into the village to buy meat by the time Bob came in for dinner at six. It was high time she swept the parlour. She would have plenty of work to fill her morning and then she could wash and change and call on Mrs North for an afternoon in town. She could change her novel at the library, go to a café for tea and cakes, look at the latest fashions in the shop-windows, have her hair done perhaps and a shampoo. She could be home about five and still have an hour in which to prepare dinner, and in the evening she and her husband might go to the cinema together or for a walk by the seaside. That had been her daily routine ever since coming to live in this new suburb five miles from Swansea.

And then it would be night, for which the daily round was but a preparation, when she and Bob would climb the stairs together and come into this room. She would sit here on the edge of the bed while he closed the heavy orange curtains, and then he would turn to her with his languid, importunate eyes and imploring hands.

Monica made a grimace of distaste. She nipped her cigarette between finger and thumb and, going to the window, leaned out to observe the street below. There was the milk-boy. Monica called to him from the window:

'Two pints. The jug's by the back door.'

Now a road in a middle-class suburb is something unique. Its character is formed and its social life completely run by women. From nine in the morning till six at night, their minions — the shopkeepers' delivery-boys, the postman with his bag, the curate and minister on their rounds, the uniformed employees of the gas and electricity companies — are the only men to be seen about the place. It is the women who determine all personal contacts between the houses; they who, by bestowing or withholding their 'good-mornings' and 'good-afternoons', decide each family's social standing. The men may hobnob with one another as they please on the train or bus on their way to and from their places of business, but when they go out with their wives of a Sunday afternoon or do the gardening under their watchful eyes on Saturdays, if one family should bump into another whom they consider inferior, great is the husbands' discomfort as they endeavour not to see each other. On those occasions they are stunned to observe the Olympian blindness of their wives and the perfect bows of their lips, their surprise turning to astonishment when one wife says just after the other has passed out of earshot:

'Did you see her new coat? Four pounds ten at the Bon Marche last week.'

Monica lit a second cigarette and gazed out at Church Road about her. This was the hour when the wives went into the village to do their daily shopping. The first to set out this morning was Mrs Clarence, a widow who lived in a house at the top end of the road, a plump, jolly and affected woman of about fifty. A heavy responsibility had fallen to her since her only daughter had married the son of the Archdeacon of Llangenith. On this account, Mrs Clarence as she walked along was looking at the windows of every house she passed, in a most judicial manner, and she stared straight at Monica without seeing her. She kept a watchful eye on the lives of all her neighbours but she greeted none save Mrs North and the two Miss Evanses. She had been at school with Mrs North, and the two sisters came of an old Newton family who had lived there before the rural village had become a populous suburb. Yet to Mrs Clarence's ears, the way the two old maids spoke, though she could not deny they were gentlewomen, was too rustic and unrefined. She had been shocked one morning to catch Lily Evans, shovel in hand, standing in the middle of the road:

'Whatever are you doing, Miss Evans?'

'Collecting this manure for the garden.'

'Oh, Miss Evans, *manure*. That's not a very nice word.'

'What should I say, *dung*?' asked Lily innocently.

'My dear Miss Evans! If you must mention it, say *droppings*. And it would be far better not to notice that such a thing is ever to be found in our road. But that's the worst of coming to live so near the country.'

On first arriving in Church Road, some four months previously, Mrs Clarence had prevailed upon the Archdeacon himself to attend her 'at home' and he had taken tea with her. The clergyman was a genial old fellow, with a body the shape of a barrel on the legs of a duck. After tea, Mrs Clarence escorted him as far as the end of the road, and as she passed some of her neighbours had said in a voice loud enough for them to hear:

'Archdeacon, I feel it's easier to put up with this street now that you have graced it.'

'Very likely,' said the barrel, and off he went on his splayed feet. Mrs Clarence's cup overflowed. The Archdeacon had done all the right things that afternoon. Later, she told the wives who came to drink her tea:

'The only thing I dreaded was that he mightn't come in his gaiters, but he did. You know, there's nothing as effective as clerical gaiters for putting neighbours in their place.'

Monica did not mind being ignored by Mrs Clarence. The widow's bliss, as well as her pride, put her outside Monica's world. But when she saw Mrs Amy Hughes following her to the shops three minutes later, Monica hid for a moment behind her curtains. She recalled the first time she had set eyes on Mrs Hughes, in one of the village shops a week after she had moved into Church Road. They had walked home together and Monica learnt that her neighbour, too, was a newcomer to the district.

'You're not from around here?' asked Mrs Hughes.

'No. From Cardiff.'

'I'm from Bangor.'

'Did you move here directly?'

'No, from Birmingham. My husband was transferred to a better position in the bank here. I expect he'll have another promotion soon. Have you decided yet which day your "at home" is to be?'

'What's that?'

'Don't you know? The afternoon you'll be at home to receive friends.'

'I don't know anyone around here,' said Monica.

'You must join the golf club. It's a most select and classy place. I've just become a member. Of course, my husband's being a cashier at the bank makes it important that I cultivate a good social circle. The last Wednesday of the month is my day. If you come over and leave some cards, I shall introduce you to some well-placed people who'll be of some help to you.'

Monica learnt, moreover, that Mrs Hughes was a graduate of the University of Wales, and being naïve she took that to be a mark of culture. Mrs Hughes had also been a schoolteacher. She was not pretty; she dressed grandly but without taste. For a fortnight the two were bosom friends. Monica began to entertain an ambition that was quite unusual for her, namely a desire for social success and going up in the world. But one morning, when the two women met in the street, Mrs Amy Hughes walked straight past her without so much as a word or smile. Monica thought it was inadvertent and called out to her. The woman did not turn round. Monica was troubled. A few days later they again came face to face and Monica stopped:

'Whatever's the matter, Mrs Hughes?'

'I beg your pardon?'

'Why do you pass me by without saying hello?'

'Oh, I'm sorry if I offend you, Mrs MacEwan, but I'm surprised that you don't understand how out of the question it is for us to be friends. I had no idea your husband was in trade. Good-morning to you.'

Monica was not lacking in dignity. She walked on without uttering a word. She had a vague but persistent idea that her own spiritual malaise was of a more aristocratic nature, after all, than the base craving of her neighbour. At least she had never paid very much attention to the whispering of others.

Can any heart know the bitterness of another? At that very moment, as she passed beneath Monica's gaze, despair was weighing heavily on the feeble shoulders of Amy Hughes. Her 'at home' had come and gone. She had spent that morning in the kitchen making pretty little pasties, and putting them flat and floury in the oven, and then taking them out again all light and golden, like the bubbles of a waterfall. She was a dab hand at making pastry. Then she had tidied her lounge, dressed, and waited for her guests to arrive. At least two or three wives of her husband's colleagues should reciprocate, for she had gone to visit them. But nobody had turned up. She and her husband had had the bitter pleasure of having to eat her handiwork. Why was she such a failure and such a pariah? So unfortunate in all her opinions and scheming? There was that Mrs Mac-Ewan; on seeing her for the first time, and noticing how elegantly she dressed, Amy Hughes had thought she would steal a march on her neighbours by making her acquaintance. Then she had heard from her husband that MacEwan was only a clock-mender in a shop with a wage of less than four pounds a week. Why aren't I more attractive? Amy Hughes complained inwardly, Why can't I dress like that Mrs Valmai Briand? There she is now coming out of her house. Why don't I have a melodious name like hers instead of Amy Hughes? I've always been held back by being shy and not forward enough. She's the one I should have greeted, not that clock-maker's wife. Mrs Briand was once a mere shop-girl, and yet now her circle of acquaintances is to be found, not among the people of Church Road, but among those living in the large houses all around us, each in its own grounds. We've been neighbours for months and we ought to say hello to each other. And when she came to do just that, — a Daimler was waiting at Mrs Valmai Briand's gate and a stout woman was sitting in it with a small fortune in squirrel's pelts draped around her shoulders, — Amy Hughes said in a loud voice, looking confidently into a face that had opened wealth's doors:

'Good-morning, Mrs Briand.'

But the cupid lips did not move, and the proud eyes under eyebrows that were like new moons swept in one contemptuous glance over the frumpish figure of Amy Hughes until it brought a blush to her forehead and neck, whereupon Mrs Valmai Briand had got into the limousine to join her fat friend.

Nor could Amy Hughes have known that it had been that very morning the bank manager had told her husband:

'Hughes, you'd better return Mrs Valmai Briand's cheque to this tailor. Briand doesn't have an account with us and she has no funds, as far as we know, with which to honour her cheque.'

Mrs North now came up the street like a schooner under full sail. There was nothing of the snob in Mrs North. Once a month, late in the evening, she filled her house with friends, got reeling drunk, and at about midnight came out into the road to see off her guests, shouting her farewells after them along the silent street, until she woke every baby and dog in the vicinity and caused cursing and the gnashing of teeth in many a heavily laden bed. Mrs North's keenest pleasure was in gossiping. Her imagination delighted in creating drama and excitement all about her. She mingled with everyone in Newton, rich and poor alike, in order to listen to her neighbours' stories, which she worked up shockingly in her own mind and then spread abroad wherever she happened to go. When Mrs Clarence reproached her for her undignified ways, she would instantly retort:

'And if I didn't chin-wag with the fishmonger's wife, what would you have to tell Mr Davies the curate this afternoon that's of any interest?'

Even now as she was making her way home, a brand-new scandal was seething in her breast. She looked about her, sniffing for someone who would listen to her. Seeing Monica at the window, she hailed her and rushed through the garden up to the house. Monica came to the door:

'Have you heard about Mrs Rosser?'

'No.'

'Thank heaven for that.'

Mrs Rosser, a young woman with a three-month-old baby, lived at the far end of Church Road. After the child's birth she had taken on a girl from the village as a daily help. On this particular morning Mrs Rosser had stayed in bed with her baby in the cot beside her. Her husband had said good-bye and left, so she thought, for his business in town. Half an hour had gone by. The fire in the bedroom was burning low and so she had rung the bell for the maid. She rang twice without getting any response. She flung on a dressing-gown and ran downstairs in her slippers to fetch some coal. The door of the back parlour was ajar and there on the sofa her husband and the maid were lying together. In her distraction Mrs Rosser had run out into the garden, where she encountered the milk-boy. 'Come here,' she shouted hysterically, pulling him into the parlour to show him the pair on the sofa. The lad had had a most glorious morning peddling the story from house to house.

'Frightful, isn't it?' said Mrs North, her eyes dancing. 'What will my friend Mrs Clarence say? She'll have to invite the Archbishop of Wales, no less, to tea, to get over the shock. But just think of that poor woman with her little baby,' — and crocodile tears came to Mrs North's eyes, — 'What would you do, Mrs MacEwan, if you were her?'

Monica laughed, the shrill, mechanical laugh she had adopted since her marriage.

'Will you be coming into town with me this afternoon?' her neighbour asked.

'No, I can't today, thanks all the same.'

'All right, good-morning. I must fly to tell my daughter all about it. It's best she hears it from me than from anyone else. You'll soon have to be thinking about the difficulties of being a mother yourself, Mrs MacEwan.'

As Mrs North went off, a small boy came up the garden path with a bundle of newspapers under his arm. Monica took her paper, closed the door and went into the lounge. She sat down at the table on which lay a half-full box of chocolates. Opening the paper, she began perusing it, reading and eating at the same time. She chewed the chocolates rather than sucked them, her jaws working vigorously. She went on turning the pages, reading a passage here, another there, the report of a child's murder, an actress's Paris divorce, an advertisement for toothpaste, another for a soap for washing silk. She did not look at the political news, nor at the report of a fire and casualties at a coal-mine in Monmouthshire, but she read the twentieth instalment of the novel, despite not having followed it up to then. It was an adventure story set among the tombs of Luxor and the pyramids of Egypt. One after the other the chocolates disappeared from the half-full box.

Monica read and pondered. What was this feeling of distaste which had been growing inside her? On returning to her own home two hours earlier, her mind had been calm enough. At last she had succeeded in relating the story that for so long had been pent up inside her, the tale of her self-justification and triumph. And already, within the space of two short hours, the story with its mixture of truth and fabrication had begun to seem pathetic enough. What would Miss Evans think of her? Well, she would not be seeing her ever again, and a wave of indignation came over Monica at the thought of that bedridden woman who had inveigled her, just as her own mother had once tried to do, into confiding her secret. Why wasn't there someone other than ailing women to give her a sympathetic hearing?

Nevertheless, Monica knew that Miss Evans was not the root cause of her depression. Slowly through the dark labyrinth of her half-formed thoughts the beast of truth was emerging into her consciousness. Several times she had noticed Mrs Rosser coming and going in the street: a tall, good-looking woman, with the effortless grace of the open air in her walk. She had seen her going out with her husband for a game of tennis or, on Sunday afternoons, with walking-stick in hand, setting out with him for a walk in the country, her bearing always eloquent of carefree health both physical and spiritual. She and her husband were surely the handsomest couple in Newton, and it was only five years since Ned Rosser had given up playing rugby for Wales. Monica thought of her now, with all her confidence in life, her two heavy breasts storing up their nourishing milk, despite the fact that she was confined to her bedroom, her control over her circumstances temporarily suspended. So fearless, so trusting as, light of foot, she ran down the stairs, and through the half-open door, without even one merciful twinge of suspicion which would have prepared her for the worst, there to find Bob and the maid together on the sofa. It is thus, in a split second, that the flesh betrays us and lays us low.

No, not Bob, of course not; but Ned Rosser. But Monica too had become unfitted for the full rituals of the flesh, and as each day passed she had become more and more so. Nor was there anything else to bind Bob MacEwan to her. The night she had told him there was life in her womb, had not his response been to let go of her and mumble, 'So we'd better not?' That was the moment she had become afraid, clutching at him and pulling him back to her in the way a miser embraces his gold. But next morning, Bob had said:

'From now on we'll have something to live for.'

The words had gone through his wife's mind like a knife. Was this how he looked upon her endeavour to fill his life, to be a mistress to him as well as a wife, utterly to satisfy and indulge his pleasure? She had turned the words over in her mind until she grasped their meaning, and understood that the monotony of love-making, and a surfeit of it, had taken root in him also. From now on her hold upon him could only slacken. Soon she would be cast aside. She too would lie, like Mrs Rosser, feeble in her bed, some strange woman would come to see to her needs, and his, and one morning she would go downstairs and look through the half-open lounge door, just as Mrs North had so maliciously hinted: 'What would you do if you were her?' It was just so that her triumph, of which she had so lately boasted, would turn to ashes in her mouth.

At the very moment this thought came to her Monica felt a sudden stab of pain in her side, sharp as a blow. It was a pain different from any she had experienced hitherto. It was like a small foot or elbow prodding inside her, and in her fright she placed her hand on the bulge. She was afraid she was going to vomit and ran up to the bedroom. Taking off her dress, she lay down under the coverlet. Gradually her pain subsided. It was thus, for the very first time ever, she was warned by the child in her womb that new claims were being made upon her, and that she had a new role in life. Listless and ill at ease, Monica slept.

She slept and she dreamt, and in one of her dreams she found herself in a large, oriental temple with many-coloured walls and pillars of granite and sandstone. At the far end, between two pillars the colour of blood, stood a chair of brilliant white marble, and on it sat Monica. She was attired in the long white

46

robe of a priestess, with sandals on her feet and heavy bracelets at her wrists. Her arms were bare and across her lap there lay a sharp sword. Two black men entered the temple from behind the throne and, between them, a prisoner in chains, his face covered by a cloth. The three walked past her to the temple's entrance. The priestess then rose from her chair and followed them, between the pillars and through the doorway. Red sandstone steps led down to an open-air platform or balcony which was atop a high rock. Monica peered over the balcony's edge and saw a wide, sandy expanse and a numberless throng gathered there and gazing up at her. The two black men stood before the crowd, the prisoner still between them, but his chains were now loosened and they dropped with a clatter about his feet. Then Monica turned to him and, raising her sword, plunged it into his breast, so that he fell down dead and hurtled over the edge into the crowd below. As he fell, his face was revealed, and Monica saw that it was Bob MacEwan.

She woke at three o'clock to hear knocking at the door. She got up irritably, put on a bed-jacket and went to see who was there. It was a gypsy with a laden basket on her arm and a little girl holding onto her skirt.

'Lady,' said the gypsy, 'you are kind to open the door to me. I've knocked at every house along the street this afternoon without getting so much as a halfpenny.'

'What do you have there?'

The gypsy slipped her basket from her arm and rested it on her hip, displaying pegs and shoelaces and feather dusters.

'I don't need any of those,' said Monica.

'What difference does that make, lady? Buy something for the sake of a poor old gypsy. Or,' — and she looked with an ingratiating smile into Monica's eyes, — 'cross my palm with silver and I'll tell you whether your child's to be a boy or a girl.'

Bristling, Monica took a step backwards.

'No thank you,' she said, and was about to close the door.

'Don't turn me away, lady. Me and the little one have had nothing to eat since early morning. Give me a sixpenny-bit now, and good luck be with you.'

'I can't afford sixpence. I'll go and get you twopence if you'll wait.'

'All right, thanks very much, and could you find something for the little girl, a toy or an apple? It'll bring you luck.'

Monica went up to her bedroom to fetch her purse. She took out two pennies. As she did so, she saw her scent-bottle on the dressing-table. Her husband had given it to her shortly after their wedding and had said jokingly as he sprayed the perfume on her hair:

'You know, don't you, that it was smelling your perfume that I first came to desire you?'

It was a phial of thin white china, skilfully made in the form of a swan. Monica recalled that she alone of her family used perfume. Hannah detested its smell so much that she had cleaned her teeth only with carbolic soap. For Monica there had always been something glamorous not only about perfumes, but about their names too, and in the pictures of the queens to be seen on their boxes — Cleopatra, Pompeia, Pompadour. She knew nothing about them. For her they were love's mistresses, beauties who had gathered about their bodies every allure of wealth and artistry for the sole purpose of captivating the hearts of their lovers. She had doted on their likenesses and imagined them sequestered from the world, walking on rose-leaves in the gardens of the Orient, or reclining on couches in the chambers of emperors, each the very incarnation of her own image of herself.

Monica snatched up the bottle and the pennies, gave the money to the woman and thrust the shiny vessel into the grubby, unperfumed hands of the little gypsy girl.

Now at last her mind was made up and for the next two hours she worked diligently. She took blankets and sheets and a mattress from the airing cupboard, and having left them a while in front of the gas fire in the lounge, spread them out on the bed in the spare room, the one her husband used as a dressing-room, though he seldom slept there. She swept and tidied the room and put a hot-water bottle in the bed. She then moved everything of her husband's out of her own room. As she worked, her mind roamed back and forth over her life. She smiled wryly as the thought occurred to her that it was while sweeping out bedrooms she had made every decision of any consequence in her life. Her ideals had developed in much the same way. On this cheap linoleum, amid the grime and floor-cloths, trod the satin shoes of Madame de Pompadour. That had been tolerable in the days when she was single, when her dreams had been set in a time that was yet to come. During the last three years trying to live at the level of soap advertisements had become more of a burden with each passing day. Monica felt a lightening of heart mixed with her bitterness when she put Bob's pyjamas on the second-hand spare bed. She gazed into her own eyes in the mirror bought at Woolworth's. She thought she could already see a difference in them, for not to feel sexual desire is to begin to die. The will-power that had kept her young had been shattered, and she expected to see creases now fast appearing, which hitherto the intensity of lust had smoothed from her forehead and chin. What was the point of persevering? Nature was stronger than she was and it was swelling and deforming her body. On marrying she had assumed that there was no danger she would have a child, for that was one of the advantages of marrying late. But she had been deceived, and she would never again have a shapely figure. She would no longer make an effort. Rather than see her hold on a much younger man grow weaker from one day to the next, it was better to give up the struggle now. Monica put the finishing touches to her arrangements. She made herself some tea, hurriedly and messily, put out food and drink for the cats, left a cold snack on the table for her husband, and went to her bed.

She heard the six o'clock bus coming to a halt at the end of the road and the male laughter of about a dozen breadwinners drawing near, Mr Briand's gate opening and closing first, casual voices bidding each other good-night, one after the other, and then the gate of her own house.

A moment passed and soon her husband's voice was calling from the bottom of the stairs:

'Hello!'

An instant later he was kneeling at her bedside:

'Are you ill, darling?'

'I was working and the baby started kicking inside me. I nearly fainted.'

'But Monica, you mustn't do any heavy work. No one in your condition does. We can get a girl from the village in. If she came just in the mornings to do some cleaning, it wouldn't cost us much.'

'No, I won't have a girl in. Promise me you won't ever bring a girl into the house, promise me, Bob.'

In her intensity, habit was greater than her resolve and her arms went tightly round his neck. Bob kissed her anxiously. She seemed old and unwell:

'Of course, if you insist.'

Monica let go of him:

'Bob, I've made up a bed for you in the spare room. You mustn't sleep with me from now on, it would be risky.'

'Shouldn't we send for the doctor?'

'Not yet, not yet. Go and have your food now. I'm sorry it's only something cold.'

He went downstairs, ate his meal, washed the day's dishes, and then came back up into the bedroom. Monica pretended to be asleep. Bob MacEwan went down again quietly lest he wake her up, turned on the gas fire in the lounge, lit his pipe and reached for the newspaper on the table. This was the first evening he had spent on his own since marrying.

Chapter Four

Bob MacEwan and Ned Rosser were sitting in the lounge bar of a public house in Swansea. It was a wet evening in late June. The six o'clock bus for Newton had long since left but for some weeks now these two had not been among its passengers. It was not on account of the story about him and the maid that Ned Rosser had stopped catching his usual bus home. His neighbours' comments did not worry him much. He had to put up with a few winks and a certain amount of drollery, and one or two said of him, 'He's a bit of a lad'. But nobody made any direct reference to his troubles. None broke the unwritten rule of the six o'clock bus. Likewise, his wife had forgiven him and they were to be seen out together as before. He had begun to blame his misfortune on the accident that had caused her to come downstairs and catch him with the maid. It was then but a small step to shifting the blame onto his wife for having come downstairs at all: 'She would have been quite happy if only she hadn't seen us'. The monotony of suburban life was getting him down. He felt the need for a change, for the excitement he had known in days gone by in the company of his rugby-playing friends. He was horrified at the thought of being seen on the six o'clock bus every day for the rest of his life. To avoid that, he would, from time to time, after finishing work in the office, call in at the comfortable bar of this pub.

One evening, at about a quarter to six, Bob MacEwan also came in. Ned Rosser had just ordered his drink and politely asked Bob what he would have:

'Whisky and soda,' said Bob.

'Missed the bus?' his neighbour asked.

'No. I didn't try to catch it.'

They sat and smoked and talked about the poor performance of the Glamorgan cricket team. Although they had seen each other daily for months now, they had never talked before. At about seven they went home together.

Meeting like this grew to be a habit with them. At first the topics they discussed were cricket and tennis and rugby and horses. Since marrying, Bob MacEwan had missed his enjoyment of sport. He was always loth to mention rugby to Monica, recalling many a conversation at the supper-table above the shop in Cardiff. On the only occasion he had ventured to suggest that she should take up tennis, there had been a row. She had made him swear that he had no regrets whatsoever about losing Hannah. Consequently, this hour spent in the company of his neighbour had afforded him, at the outset, the kind of pleasure playing truant gives a schoolboy: it was a pleasant, risk-free act of treachery. He never tired of listening to Ned Rosser's reminiscences. Ned enjoyed the admiration and the simple flattery Bob paid him.

There was, moreover, something deeper that drew them to each other. Neither asked the other the polite questions that were to be heard on the bus: 'How's the family? How's Mrs MacEwan?'. As Ned Rosser once put it:

'Those fellows on the bus can't forget even for half an hour that they've got family responsibilities. They tell one another dirty stories sometimes, the way their children dream up fairy-tales, because there's no other means of escape in their lives.'

He suddenly turned to Bob and said boldly:

'You know, there's nothing more certain to make a man old than being too happy at home.'

Bob realized that this was not a general statement but a confession and an invitation. He asked:

'Do you believe in living dangerously?'

'Don't you? Life's a game, and I know how it's played.'

'You're luckier than I am,' Bob replied pensively.

This June evening Bob MacEwan was in spiritual turmoil. He quickly drained his glass and ordered a second and a third, urging his companion to do the same.

'What's the hurry?' the latter asked. 'Something bothering you?'

'Everything.'

Ned Rosser laughed:

'Don't worry so much. Learn to take things easy. I make it a rule, if things are going badly in the office or at home, to put an extra two bob on a horse that's running that day. That's how I shift my anxiety onto something I find interesting. Often it's those horses that win for me.'

'Listen, Ned.'

'Yes?'

'It's awful for a man to talk about his wife . . . .'

'Cut out the middle-class hypocrisy, will you? Man to man, now. If you need advice, don't beat about the bush.'

Bob remained silent for a moment. He emptied his glass and ordered another. Then he asked:

'D'you think a woman can be so resentful of the child she's carrying in her womb that she'd want to die in order to kill it?'

Ned Rosser gave a low, uncomfortable whistle. This was not what he had been expecting.

'Is that how things are?'

'I don't know. I'm trying to use my imagination, to make a

guess. It's beyond me. She hasn't got out of bed these last two months.'

'Why don't you ask a doctor to see her?'

'If I mention it, she flies into a rage.'

'Is she really ill?'

'I'm afraid so.'

'How much longer has she got to go?'

'Another two months. She's not making any preparations or sewing anything, and if I dare say something hopeful about the baby, she lets me have it. I've tried two or three times to get her interested by bringing home a nursing magazine, — you know, for young mothers describing the right clothes and so on. It was enough to make her very angry.'

'You'd better send for a doctor without asking her. It's dangerous for her to be on her own all day in the seventh month.'

'I know.'

An uneasy silence grew between them. This was not the way they usually talked. Then suddenly Ned Rosser said:

'What causes all this is the unnatural way in which we middle-class people live. Our idea of marriage is to take a young man and woman away from their families and isolate them, each inexperienced couple on their own, leaving them to work out their own marital salvation as best they can. And heaven help the young couple who get themselves talked about. Each household has to keep the lid down tight on its own boiling cauldron, so that sometimes we have no alternative but to explode. I often think that the working-class life of the slums, with half-a-dozen families sharing the same house and being involved in one another's troubles all higgledy-piggledy, is a more normal and human way of living than what goes on in our rows of well-kept purgatories, each with a garden of flowers at the front.'

He got to his feet in a foul temper, regretting his outburst, for having said so much all at once.

'Well, are you coming home?'

'It's early yet.'

'It's later than usual. Put two bob on the race tomorrow afternoon. Good-night now.'

He hurried out, like someone in need of fresh air.

Bob ordered another drink. So, he thought, I've gone and upset the only one whose company has helped me keep my mind off things.

But what was there to go home to? To make a meal for himself and Monica? To sweep and clean, as best he could, the rooms downstairs? What about her room? No, he had better not think of that for the time being. What if he'd told Ned Rosser how he spent his evenings? Bob smiled bitterly as he imagined his neighbour's expression. What had first made him take half an hour off in this quiet pub had been the need for a little rest after the day's work before going home to face a different kind of work. In those early days he had no misgivings about Monica's behaviour. He had praised her good sense in refusing to do any hard work, in lying down and taking things easy. He had noticed, indeed, that she had been taciturn and undemonstrative, but Monica had always been a moody one. He would have preferred her to take on a maid to help her, but as she had rejected that suggestion, he was content to buy food on his way home from town, to cook it later, and do all he could to keep the house clean and orderly. Often during the first fortnight he had asked her:

'Did you get up today?'

'No.'

Another time:

'Are you sure you're being sensible? Those doctors' books say you should walk about a bit every day and do some light work . . . . Are you hungry?'

'Yes.'

Bob watched her eating. As she did so, there was something

of her old vitality in her manner. He realized as she devoured the meat that she had eaten nothing since morning. Next day, before setting off for work, he made some sandwiches for her and put them with chocolate and milk and a jug of water on the dressing-table by the bed. That too became a habit with them.

One evening Bob brought home some wood and after dinner set about measuring and sawing it in the kitchen. Monica called to him:

'What are you doing?'

'I've bought some wood and started making a cradle for the baby. I've got the instructions for making a terrific one. Here they are.'

Monica turned away irritably:

'You mustn't. I can't stand the sound of planing and sawing. To me it's like the sound of a coffin being made.'

Bob tried to make light of it:

'There's a lot of difference between a cradle and a coffin.'

'Not as far as I'm concerned.'

'But Monica, we have to do something. You won't sew, and we can't afford to buy everything at the last minute.'

'Don't worry. You won't have to buy anything. But I can't stand the sound of that sawing.'

Bob recalled reading an article in which a doctor said the shock of pregnancy and childbirth was as severe for some women as shell-shock was to soldiers in wartime. I shall have to remember that, he thought, and show some sympathy for her. The weeks dragged by.

Bob MacEwan was uncomfortable in the presence of pain. He would, if need be, punish himself rather than hurt others. This hyper-sensitivity was part of his soft carnality. Monica knew that, and took advantage of it. She had discovered that by tormenting herself she was able to make his life a nightmare, so that not a moment passed without her pitiful image coming

57

into his mind. In slackening her earlier hold on him she had found a new way of binding him to her.

'Bob, tidy this bed for me.'

He recalled that, when they first got their own house, Monica had been willing to spend money only on furniture for her own bedroom. The rest of their rooms were stark and poorly furnished, but she bought a bed, a wardrobe, and a dressing-table made of walnut. She spread deep Persian rugs on the floor. For the large double bed she chose fine Irish linen with hand-stitched hems. An eiderdown made blue-green waves over the blankets, complementing the orange of the long curtains at the window. But it was in her choice of nightdresses and pyjamas that Monica satisfied her romantic soul. Bob could well recall the night she had first worn them, trying on one wonder after another before his eyes, each splendid garment shining and rustling all over her body.

'Will you choose the one you'd like me to wear on this first night?'

'Monica, you've spent more on these than on the rest of the house put together, and I'll be the only one to see you in all your glory.'

'I dress and live for you, only for you. Nobody else is to imagine what sort of woman your wife is. Tell me, aren't I a match for Cleopatra?'

'If you want me to make the bed, you'll have to get up,' said Bob as he plumped up the cushions of the easy-chair ready for her.

'No, better not, just tidy the blankets.'

He pulled the bedclothes off her. The feather mattress had sunk into a hollow in its middle and the edges were sticking up uncomfortably all round her. Crumbs and bits of food had accumulated thickly under her hips and feet. The bedsheet and pillow were grimy and torn. They, and her nightdress, too, were sticky with fat. There were vomit stains on the blankets and on the rug at the foot of the bed. Her legs had turned a dark colour and were swollen, and there were sweaty patches under her chin and on her neck and breasts. Monica lay, heavy and motionless, in the midst of the stench.

Bob looked round at the room. There was nothing that had not been defiled.

'Monica, there's an awful smell in here. You had a rule once that the cats were never allowed into this room. Can't you at least stop them making a mess?'

'I've got to have some company, haven't I? If you don't want them to make a mess, put a box in the corner with soil and ashes in it. I can't do without the cats now.'

For a moment Bob suspected that she was enjoying the sensation of seeing his unhappiness. Then, as he contemplated her unkempt, unhealthy-looking body, he cried in shock and bewilderment:

'I'll have to clean up in here. Can I start by giving you a wash?'

But all she would let him do was change the sheets and take out the rugs to shake them:

'Why are you going to all this bother?'

'But this room, Monica, this bed, and your body that used to be all scented. How can you put up with the stink?'

What he failed to realize was that the bedroom which had once been Monica's temple, the bed she had made her altar, even her own limbs, were no more than means to an end, and now that they had lost their purpose she was able to view their defilement with equanimity. Although very emotional, Bob MacEwan could not understand passion. Even in the days of their sexual bliss on this large bed, he had wondered sometimes at the lyricism of his wife, the way her imagination embroidered the simple sexual act. A less exigent kind of love-making would often have suited the ordinary clay of which Bob was made, though he never learned to be indifferent to Monica's touch. Even now, had she reached out towards him from amidst her squalor . . . .

Bob ordered another drink.

'I've got to keep my nerves under control. Only two months to go.'

He was tired and he was afraid. Oh, if only there were someone to lay a kind, soothing hand on his temples. The cruellest part of his wife's behaviour was that she was so undemonstrative towards him. In days gone by, whenever she had sat with him, reading the newspaper at the fireside, her foot would touch his or her arm would be on his shoulder, her fingers playing now and then with the lobe of his ear. Not even the reports of Rowe Harding's feats on the rugby-field could make him forget, of a Saturday evening, just how tender was the palm of her hand. But for weeks now, those incontinent hands had lain motionless and dirty on the blankets, like rusty weapons cast aside. Just when he had expected the tenderness of arm, eye and lip to increase, and the communion of the flesh to discover a subtler, more indirect means of expression, Bob found himself cast out and rejected. She would only squint sidelong at him. The tone of her voice when she addressed him was accusing and rancorous. She made no attempt to hide her squalor. She laughed defiantly whenever he noticed some new uncleanliness that was worse than usual. The cats were no longer allowed out of her room. When he alighted from the bus at the end of the road he usually saw one of them basking in the sun on the windowsill. He would feel the urge to wring that cat's neck. Once, after cleaning out the box of ashes, he had asked:

'Monica, shouldn't we have these cats put down?'

'Yes, of course — after I've gone.'

And she clasped one of them to her bare bosom under the bed-clothes.

Bob MacEwan abandoned himself to self-pity. He failed to notice that two women sitting in another corner of the bar were observing him with interest. In the way of all ineffectual men, he went over and over the wrong and injustice that had been done him. It was not fair of Monica. She had let him down. He had sacrificed so much for her sake, and got no thanks for it. Even these last few weeks he had been putting aside part of his wages against the time of the birth. He opened his wallet and counted four pound notes. He would call at the bank tomorrow to pay them into his account. But when he had boasted to Monica of his thrift, she only laughed:

'Keep them for your next honeymoon.'

Her only pleasure was in hurting him, taking her pain out on him. It was in order to injure and insult him, he thought, that she defiled everything for which he had regard. It was the fruit of his body that she was mistreating in her womb. He thought how Hannah would have behaved if she had become pregnant: the light that would have shone in her eyes, her few proud, delicate words of love and gratitude to the husband who had enriched her, her heartfelt commitment to her motherhood. Yes, how a woman behaves when pregnant is the ultimate test of her spirit. Had he married Hannah he would surely by now have his own shop. Hannah was a first-class business woman. But this other woman had come between them and ruined his life. She was turning his home into a tip for cats. Oh, if only she were to die. Perhaps she would. Then he would be free. He could start again, put the nightmare of the last few months behind him. Forget, forget. If he could have just one night of respite from his worry, one night of complete irresponsibility, and lose himself in welcoming arms.

The man who wallows in self-pity is ready to be cruel to others; there is, moreover, a fine line between self-pity and wantonness. Bob called for another whisky. He no longer tried to restrain his imagination from toying with the thought that Monica might die. The thought ceased to frighten him. He had a right to her death, to his own freedom. She it was who had first stirred the wildest sexual urges in his nature, she who over the years had nurtured them. Does not every woman who is loved select and summon to permanent life those elements in her lover which bind him to her? It was thus Monica had gradually killed the Bob who had once been loved by Hannah, and raised in his stead a man formed in the image of her own imagination. It was a sign of her victory that his lust, his body's craving for her little tricks and favours, had survived the will that had shaped it. He was her creation, the man who now sat in this pub wanting her death, eyed by the two women who had been watching him for an hour and assessing his readiness to be ensnared and carried off.

He felt an intense urge to punish Monica. Much though she had suffered up to now, it had been as a consequence of her own surliness. Nor would her death make proper amends for the humiliation she had inflicted on him. If she were to die without his once paying her back, even her death would be a last gesture of indifference. It was stupid of him to be so tender towards her. Until this evening he had never lingered even for so much as an hour after finishing his day's work without hurrying home to wait upon her. Now at last that was all over. She would taste the medicine of neglect.

I'm so lonely, thought Bob, and that too is her doing. Since marrying, he had been without friends. Monica had never invited anyone to their home. She had not felt the need for friends. In the old days he and Hannah had been members of a tennis club, gone to dances and bridge-parties, and had a wide circle of acquaintances of both sexes. Monica had been jealous, not so much of women as of men, of anyone who claimed a part in her husband's life. She had insisted on his turning his back on the world to share with her the ceaseless, monotonous drama of passionate love. In the end she had managed to detach him from every ordinary, healthy pleasure. Then, after succeeding in this, she had brought the play to an abrupt end and quit the stage, leaving it for the cats to defile. Bob thought bitterly how foolish it was for anyone who seeks happiness to put all his eggs in one basket. Being unfaithful, as Ned Rosser had suggested, that is the key to happiness.

'Ten o'clock, gentlemen, time please.'

Bob MacEwan looked up. He had not noticed that the bar was so crowded. There it was again, — even in a room full of men chatting to one another, Monica had put the chain of her own loneliness around him so that he was unable to break free of her influence. Only at this last moment, with the customers dispersing and bidding their polite good-nights to the landlady, did he become aware of just how lonely he was. He put on his hat, got to his feet, picked up his glass, drained it, and muttered to himself:

'Damn and blast her!'

He was answered by the skittish laughter of a young woman passing by:

'Not me, I hope?'

He looked at her in surprise:

'Did I say that aloud?'

'Well, you must be head over heels in love. Did she let you down, after you've been waiting all night for her? Shame on her.'

'Now, gentlemen, out you go, if you please. You can carry on talking outside. I have to close now.'

'Really, you didn't ought to curse her like that. Poor thing, how d'you know who stopped her coming, some other sweet-heart, two perhaps. A woman's life is a terrible thing. Come on, give us a smile. You've been brooding something awful all evening, I wanted to put my arms around you to comfort you. But I'll bet a bob you never saw so much as my shoe?'

'No, I didn't, not until you spoke to me just now.'

'There we are then, you owe me a bob. Well, buck up, it isn't the end of the world. Will I do instead? But fair play, you haven't seen anything of me yet. The only time you've looked up at all was when you were ordering more drinks. Wait until we're under that lamp and I'll undo my coat for you to see. Now, look. Aren't I every bit as good as her?'

'You're very pretty.'

'Pretty, you say. Is that all? You're very stingy with your compliments. That way, to the left. Give me your arm. There, you're laughing now. D'you know, you look ten years younger already. This is the house. I've got a key. You'll have to follow me because I know where the light-switch is. Here we are. Isn't it a pretty little place? As pretty as me? Now, what'll you have, another whisky?'

Bob MacEwan woke at midnight to the chiming of an unfamiliar clock. He opened his eyes in a brightly lit room, — the light had not been switched off. There was a strange arm under his head. He sobered up in one terrifying second, and leapt off the bed:

'I've got a wife waiting for me.'

He did not listen to the woman's cheeky reply. Wild with agitation and shock, he put on his clothes and soon the door of the house had closed behind him and he was out in the street. He ran towards the main road. Not until he reached it did he slacken his pace.

The night was summery and clear, and the city streets quiet

beneath its enchantment. Hat in hand, Bob felt a slight, fresh breeze ruffle his hair and cool the crown of his head. He grew calmer. His agitation subsided and his heart stopped racing. He began to walk with a lighter step. He filled his lungs with the cool air and then emptied them with a long sigh. The peace of a healthy, satisfied body came over him. Suddenly he laughed aloud.

'I'll take a taxi home. I'll get one by the station. It'll cost me another ten bob but I'll be home in twenty minutes.'

He put his hand in the pocket of his coat for one of the three remaining pound notes. He rummaged for it. His wallet was not there. He went through all his pockets, and his fingers ferreted over his clothes. His wallet had gone.

Giddy and faint, Bob sat on the steps of the post office. What could he do? Go back to the house and accuse the woman? On reflection he realized that he had no idea how to find her. He could retrace his steps to the street where she had taken him, but he had not made a note of the house's number, all he could remember was that it was one of a row. If he knocked, no one would open the door. Nor did he dare tell a policeman of his plight.

He stood up at last. He had eight miles to walk and his footsteps began to echo once more through the empty streets. For the first half-hour of his trek a multitude of ideas, intentions, doubts, fears, pursued one another through his mind. There was no end to his wretchedness. Did not life bear him some particular malice? Should he drown himself tonight and put an end to his worries on the terrible rocks of Gower? Or stay out all night and in the morning draw his savings from the bank and take a train to London and disappear? Go home and sneak into his wife's bedroom and smother her in her sleep? 'I'm going off my head,' Bob whispered to himself pitifully, unable to put these bogeys out of his mind. But his feet continued on their way, and gradually all his cares sank into his shoes. The apathy of fatigue now came over him. He gave up thinking. Only on reaching the outskirts of Newton did his consciousness stir again. How would he get into the house? What would he say to Monica? Would she be awake? He was too weary to care. To sleep, to sleep for a long time. It was three in the morning when he put his key in the door.

He took off his shoes and went upstairs in his stockinged feet.

'Bob?'

Her voice was tremulous. Bob went in to her. He could see that she was weeping.

'I was sure you'd gone, left me.'

'No, no, my love. I was held up until midnight seeing to some compasses for a ship that's sailing at first light, and I missed the last bus, so I had to walk all the way home.'

'Bob, don't leave me to die on my own. Oh, I was afraid. Afraid.'

Bob undressed. He too was weeping from fatigue and nervous exhaustion and her unexpected welcome. A moment later he threw himself into bed beside her, into the midst of the squalor. They fell asleep in each other's arms.

Chapter Five

Next day, after her husband had gone to work, Monica got up.
Though unsteady on her feet, she put on a bed-jacket and sat
in the armchair. Every now and again she would gingerly walk
around the room. She also massaged her legs in an attempt to
ease the swelling and bring back their circulation. She spent
hours rubbing and exercising them, and whenever she grew
tired she would lie down for a while and then start all over
again.

The following morning she said to Bob:

'Don't cut me any bread and butter today. I'll go down
myself.'

He could hardly believe his ears:

'Are you sure you can manage, darling?'

'I'll have to learn.'

What Bob understood by that was: I shall have to learn to
be content, like other wives. He therefore set off for work in a
happier frame of mind than he had known for two months,
and hurried home on the six o'clock bus. Monica had gone to
bed, but she had washed and there was a clean tablecloth laid
in readiness for his dinner. Later on she heard him singing as
he washed the dishes. That done, he came up to the bedroom.
The ash-box was gone from its usual corner. Surprised, Bob
asked:

'Where are the cats?'

'I was chatting with the milk-boy today. He was complaining about mice in the dairy. So I offered him the cats and he took them away this afternoon.'

Bob did not know what to say. Her voice was hard and warning him not to embrace her. A few moments later, Monica asked:

'Can you come home on time tomorrow?'

'Yes, I think so. Why?'

'I think I'm strong enough now to go out for a stroll. Will you come with me tomorrow evening?'

Bob promised, but his happiness was not unalloyed. There was an element of apprehension in it. He would have liked to deceive himself that Monica regretted her behaviour and was now mending her ways in an effort to win back his affection. She had confessed that she had been terrified the night she thought he had left her: the change in her had begun the following morning. It would have been wonderful to think that this was a victory for him, that the rod was at last in his hands. After all, if he was going to be a father and head of a family, it was fitting that he should prove himself master. He did not love her any the less for having got the better of her. Maybe he loved her more: there was in his love that particle of half-contempt or pity, or perhaps submission, which renders perfect the love that is felt by men. These days Bob felt a great need of reasons for respecting himself.

But he could not be sure. Although Monica had changed, she did not start to show him affection. When they woke up in each other's arms that morning, she had been as much ashamed as he. She had not reached out for him afterwards. Bob was determined to stifle his misgivings. At least she had asked him to take her out.

The following evening it was nine o'clock before Bob came home. Tired of waiting for him, Monica was sitting in the easy chair in her bedroom.

'I'm very sorry,' Bob said, 'but there was nothing I could do about it. The shop isn't mine, you know, and I couldn't refuse to stay on to finish a job.'

'Don't worry. It's not at all important.'

Monica answered quite casually, but Bob was agitated. He looked pale and ill at ease.

'You work late far too often,' she said to him with a half-smile.

'How else can we pay our way?'

He was on the point of falling out with her. Monica stood up to go to her bed.

'Will tomorrow evening do?'

'Of course, if you like, and if you're free.'

Ever since marrying, Bob and Monica had been in the habit of telling each other white lies. In the days of their love-making it had been convenient, an innocuous way of thrusting aside any fact that might have been an obstacle to a rapid immersion in the pleasures of the flesh. On the lie's being subsequently detected, they were not peeved with each other, but would laugh irresponsibly like children. Now, with the climate changed, their awareness of each other's lying had taken a dangerous turn. Monica knew that working late was a lie. Bob knew that she knew, and was angry with her because she did not conceal it. She sulked because she was consumed by unsatisfied curiosity.

Next evening Bob arrived home punctually. But now it was his turn to show reluctance:

'Must we go out? Wouldn't it be nicer to sit in the garden?'

'I particularly want to go for this walk.'

'Where shall we go?'

'The cemetery.'

Now the cemetery is the most agreeable spot in Newton. It lies in a low meadow with wooded slopes on three sides. This meadow was once the bed of a river, but the river sank into its limestone bed, so that all that now remains is a cave or two on the lower slopes. The small enclosure faces south and is sheltered from the winds. A flower-garden has been planted around the chapel which stands at its entrance, and from there up to the northern end there runs a path, neatly lined with yew-trees on both sides, which divides it down the middle, leading the visitor's gaze from the chapel up to the far end where oak, ash and elm trees spread their branches for the birds. Between these two rows of yew, standing like black columns amidst the graves' marble crosses, walk the mourners and the coffins bedecked with flowers are carried to their final resting-places. Here too, on Sunday and holiday afternoons, young men and women stroll arm in arm, and young mothers push their prams. On some of the children's graves near the path there are small white marble angels, and sometimes a three-year-old girl will leave her mother's side and run between the yews to plant a warm kiss on the angel's cupid lips.

'Do you remember the last time we came this way?' asked Bob.

'Palm Sunday, wasn't it?'

On that Sunday the cemetery had been more of a garden than usual. All the previous day, and from early on Sunday morning, men and women had been busy tidying the graves, removing weeds and decorating the burial-ground with narcissi and tulips and daffodils. By the afternoon hundreds had congregated there, as they always did, some to enjoy the view and many who had come long distances to put a bunch of flowers on the family grave. Rich and poor, the rustic villagers of Newton and expensively clad women alighting from sleek limousines, were to be seen side by side arranging flowers and trimming the grass. This is an old custom which has survived all the revolutions of South Wales, and although there is scarcely anyone on Palm Sunday afternoon who whispers the *memento etiam Domine* now, yet the hands move tenderly and reverently at their task, as if they at least remember and implore. That afternoon Monica said:

'I'd have liked my mother to be buried here. I'd have had a grave of my own then.'

There were two ways of getting from Church Road to the cemetery gate. The path across the field was just under two hundred yards. But Monica insisted on going by the main road, which was more than half a mile. This is the route the hearse will take, she said to herself. She walked slowly. Her feet were too big for her shoes. She leaned heavily on her husband's arm. At the gate, she stood and gazed for a while up the path between the rows of yew-trees. The cemetery lay in shadow, the thick woods on the slopes hiding the sun in the west. They were alone in the silence. Bob shivered suddenly. She disengaged her arm from his.

'I shouldn't like to be here on my own in the middle of the night,' he said, trying to be light-hearted.

'Why? Do you believe in ghosts?'

'I don't know, but I shouldn't like to, all the same, in case I happened to see something.'

'That wouldn't frighten me. It would be more frightening to be here in the middle of the night with nothing astir and nothing to be seen.'

'The birds aren't singing now.'

'Let's go up the path.'

They walked slowly between the yews. Monica looked about her. They came to the unused part of the cemetery at the far end. Monica stood still.

'Will you bury me here, at this very spot?'

Bob lost his temper.

'Please, Monica, don't be silly. I've had enough of your senseless talk. I shall die before you yet.'

She answered with deliberation:

'Don't be angry. I'm quite serious. It's true these last few months I've neglected myself. But even if I hadn't, I wouldn't come through this. You don't know how old I am.'

'What d'you mean?'

'I'm nearly forty. My mother had two other children between me and Hannah, both of them stillborn.'

Bob did not know what to say. For a moment their minds went back to their first days together:

'You were a very innocent young lad then.'

She went on, calmly:

'Listen. You must try to understand me now. I'm going to try to tell you the truth. You think I've been sulking these last two months because I'm going to have a baby. Perhaps you think I was angry with you. It wasn't that. It was life I was angry with. I'd made plans. I'd won you and decided to keep you for myself. Without sharing you with anyone else. I thought I could. Without making any preparations for the most natural thing in the world. Even when I found I was pregnant, I thought for a while that I could make that another rope to bind you to me. Then, the day you went to Cardiff, everything became clear to me. I saw that I'd already failed. I realized not only that my body had changed and I was never going to get my figure back, but that even if it were not so, it wasn't my looks, or my love either, that had been binding you to me all this time, only laziness and habit. I remembered what you said when I told you how it was with me. To be fair, it wasn't your fault that I'd deceived myself for so long. That was the day I decided to give up. I wouldn't go on trying to charm you or satisfy you. You could go free. That was what I thought. But alas, I didn't really know myself. I started neglecting my body and clothes and the bed in order to drive you away from me. Before very long, I could see that it worried you and was bringing you back to me in a new way, and before I half-realized it I was enjoying persecuting you and hurting you and making you anxious about me. Exactly the same enjoyment, you remember, as when I used to sleep with you. All I could think of was new tricks to tire you and occupy your thoughts. Habit had come to dominate me. Up until the night you stayed away from me, that is. I had a shock that night. I wasn't afraid of losing you. It wasn't what you thought at all. But I realized once again what had happened to me. I could see that I could neither leave you alone nor give you up. I had no control over it. That's what frightened me. I was afraid because I knew it had to come to that and I couldn't face it. That night I began weeping like a child. You came into bed with me. And next morning I started to learn a new lesson. It's odd, but I've been lonely all my life. I had no chance to be like other people; and yet I could never accept it as something that has to be borne. I couldn't face it. I had to have my fantasies in order to fill the emptiness inside me. And when you came into my life, you didn't rescue me from those fantasies, I involved you in them. For me you were a plaything. I never loved you honestly. It was Hannah who loved you. But I couldn't leave you alone. And I knew I never should unless I went with you to choose my grave and tell you the truth as we stood before it. This is where I'll have to leave you in peace, and then you won't have to worry if I soil my nightdress.'

Monica laughed her old, unnatural, high-pitched laugh, and its echo was flung back at them over the graves by the rocky slopes, all around them.

'Come home,' Bob said, in a whisper. He was sure now that Monica had taken leave of her senses and that her illness had affected her mind.

'Yes, let's go home. We can take the path across the field now.'

'Monica, may I send for the doctor tomorrow?'

'Yes, if you like.'

They set off. Monica trudged more heavily than before, as if the cemetery's clay were already clinging to her feet.

The village doctor called the following afternoon. Bob had been to see him on his way to work. Monica opened the door to him and went back to bed, and he followed her upstairs as soon as he heard that she was ready. He asked a good many questions, examining her carefully, and his face grew more and more serious as he proceeded.

'Mrs MacEwan,' he said at last, 'I'll come back this evening to give my diagnosis to your husband and talk things over with him. I have to tell you that your condition is somewhat unsatisfactory. You should have come to see me four months ago. Now then, what we must do is arrange for you to go into a private hospital in town. Will you agree to that?'

'To what, Doctor?'

'Perhaps we can help you with a small, quite simple operation. Are the pains in your back and legs quite bad?'

'Yes, they are.'

'If you'll come into town tomorrow, I'll get a second opinion. We must do all we can for you, and without delay. Perhaps it would be prudent if we took this baby away from you. I don't yet really know.'

In the doctor's cautious words Monica heard the verdict on her. She was quick enough to understand when he said he detected the symptoms of dropsy.

As the doctor left, he said:

'When will Mr MacEwan be home?'

'He said he'd probably be late tonight, because he's working until seven. He'll be here by eight.'

'All right, I'll come back at about nine o'clock. By then perhaps I'll have arranged a bed for you. Good-afternoon.'

Monica listened to him going down the stairs, closing the

front door, treading the gravel path, shutting the garden-gate and the door of his motor-car; she heard the engine start and the car moving off down the road, the horn sounding as it turned the corner, and then the vehicle accelerating into the distance, its noise fading and then becoming lost on that blurred boundary between a murmur and silence, in which the silence is not something new but an endless extension of the murmur itself. At certain intense moments in life the human ear is so finely tuned that it hears one particular sound that retains its significance long after it has faded away, and then the silence of that sound as a special, discrete element of the general silence into which it has merged, and it is a long while before the two become one complete silence.

It was thus Monica listened to the doctor's car. Later, — in another five minutes perhaps, — she would have to face the significance of what he had told her, the terrible, implicit threat. For the moment her ears were straining with the effort of coping with the shock of the visit: in this way, sometimes, the large buffers in a railway terminus retract in order to cushion the impact of the engine that has been shunted too rapidly into its resting position.

There was nothing in what the doctor had to say that she did not already know. She could guess the meaning of the unusually large swellings which were giving her pain. She knew they contained her death. Had she not turned to death as to a new bridegroom? She had renounced not only love-making and sexual desire but persecution and hatred too. She had even taken her leave of lying. By what discipline had she learned at last to deny herself the vacuous fantasies that had been a veil between her and the nothingness of existence? Only the previous evening she had chosen her own grave. She had gazed at the earth that would in a short while cover her, gazed at it until she could see down into the oaken box where her eyes would soon be worm-eaten holes, and the brain that had been working

75

behind them would rot into a little wet mess at the base of the skull. She had contemplated all this, and held it before her eyes long enough to feel her blood run cold and her personality, her sensuality and her will-power shrivelling and withering into a little heap of dust at her feet. What further terrors could the doctor inspire in her breast after that?

A lie. Deception and a lie. Monica had thought that she had two months' peace of mind. Without her realizing it, these two months of life had sustained her audacity and reinforced her resolution and self-discipline. As long as she had these two months it had been easy for her to take her husband's arm and walk with him along that path on which he would in due course escort her bier. Having these two months before her, she had relished her melodramatic speech in the cemetery and enjoyed her husband's obvious embarrassment and the clarity of her own vision and the trenchancy of her words. Two months was an indefinite, extended period. It was how many? — eight or nine weeks perhaps, sixty days with twenty-four hours to each. To an ordinary, normal mind, the speed at which it would pass was only slightly more comprehensible, a little more terrible, than if it had been ten years. No one takes fright on hearing that he has only ten more years to live. Our feeble minds cannot continue for more than a few minutes in a state of terror. We are such children that we soon transform the ultimate fear, so long as we can put a bit of distance between us and it, into mental amusement. A thousand and one things could happen during the course of two months. While her final agony was still a full two months off, Monica had taken pleasure in observing herself, playing with the thought of her own end, just as novelists and poets toy with it, weaving their pseudo-profound sentences around it and their most pompous, dishonest figures of speech. In this way a murderer who has been condemned to hang will appeal to a higher court against the sentence. He does not think his appeal will succeed, but he consoles himself nevertheless: Nothing can happen to me before the verdict; and the date of the hearing, together with all the rigmarole of preparing for it, becomes a veil between him and everything that may follow. Having failed there, he urges his lawyer to make a direct appeal for clemency to the Home Secretary; he will have forms to fill in, his solicitor and family to consult. Thus between him and the substantial fact of the scaffold there is still an uncertain, unspecific respite during which anything, and perhaps — who knows? — the one unbelievable, unexpected, but intensely desirable thing might happen. In that rich interval, which passes so quickly for everyone outside the cell but stretches like miser's gold for the condemned murderer, he is gulled into enjoying the spectacle of his own calamitous fate, his exceptional position between life and death, even the comings and goings and the consultation and whispering all about him, the visits from his family and the chaplain's solemn talk. A man's inexhaustible ability to lose himself in dreams and fantasies, his ability to turn everything that happens to him into a drama for his own entertainment, becomes a wall between him and terror. It is probably in the wondrous excitement and uncertainty of those hours that he experiences life at its sweetest. Then, one evening, just as he has tidied his cell's narrow bed and is wondering what further developments there might be in his case on the morrow, the governor of the prison comes in and says: 'Tomorrow, at eight o'clock in the morning, you are to be hanged'. The news is so unexpected, his shock so terrible, that it is as if he had never been sentenced to hang until now. It was thus, completely without warning, in the midst of her play-acting, that Monica had been trapped.

So easily had she fallen into the snare. She had let Bob send for the doctor out of a wish to convince herself that she no longer cared what might happen to her. In that moment of vanity and spiritual pride she had surrendered control of her own life and put herself irresponsibly into the hands of others. She soon had to pay for it. Next morning she would be taken away and put to lie in a narrow bed under an unfamiliar roof, she would hear once more the clink of medicine bottles, doctors in their white coats would stand around her as she had once before seen them bending over her mother's body, the chloroform mask would be put over her mouth and nostrils and she would be told to breathe in and count one, two, three, four . . . . She would lose consciousness and the darkness would engulf her. Monica was sure that she would not awaken from the chloroform. Or if she did, it would be, like her mother before her, only to suffer the final agony.

Monica got out of bed. She dared not lie there quietly thinking of tomorrow. What half-an-hour ago had been far enough away had now become tonight and tomorrow. Even now the doctor would be in town arranging a bed for her. Terror is mute and shapeless. The skull and grave are but the playthings and bogeys of the imagination. It is not they which inspire terror but the last minutes, the ceasing to be. She began to reason: But I'm not all that ill. If I must die, why can't I stay calm till the very last moment? Do they want to take away from me my last few weeks just to save the life of this child? It's not fair, it's not right. Oh, if only Bob were here, or my mother. She dragged herself clumsily about the house, from room to room, arranging a chair here, a bowl there, searching wildly for small, comforting, everyday chores in an attempt to convince herself that the doctor's visit had been a dream and nothing in her world had changed. She went into her husband's bedroom and began going through his clothes, tidying them and getting out for mending some of his shirts that had been damaged in the laundry. She fondled them tenderly. She remembered the afternoon she had bought this cravat to go with his blue suit, the morning she had chosen that silk dressing-gown for his birthday. Every drawer in the chest bore testimony to their life together.

Monica pressed a pair of his pyjamas to her cheek. These garments belonged so intimately to her daily routine that there was something in them of friendly warmth and consolation. A tear rolled from her eye onto the white cotton. The stillness of the house was hideous to her. She closed the drawer noisily to break the silence, but the sound only served to deepen it all about her and it jarred on her nerves even more. She tugged at another drawer, the small one in the upper part of the chest, where her husband's handkerchiefs and collars were kept. The drawer would not open. She tugged a second time. It was locked. That was odd: Bob was not in the habit of locking anything, and much less would he lock it and remove the key. Her curiosity had been aroused. She went to look for her own bunch of keys. She was glad of something to take her mind off tomorrow. She would have to keep herself occupied until Bob came home, not give her fear a chance, fill her mind. She wondered whether she could not call on Mrs North again, or Miss Evans.

What, she wondered, was Bob keeping under lock and key? She smiled as she imagined him putting together a few small things for the baby, some napkins perhaps or a shawl, and hiding them away so innocently in the drawer lest she should see them and be angry with him. She had been so foolish to refuse the gifts of life. If only she could start all over again she would sew and fill the drawers to welcome the new life within her. She wondered whether the baby would live after being taken out of her. That was quite possible in the seventh month. No, she must not think of that. She tried her keys in the drawer. At last she found one that fitted, and after being forced a little, the lock gave way. She opened the drawer. There was neither shawl nor layette. The crisp collars lay neatly in the nearest corner. Behind them the handkerchiefs were arranged in two rows, the coloured ones on the left and the plain white ones to the right. Monica could make out the initials R.M. that she had embroidered in their corners. So why had the drawer been locked? She pulled it right out, and there, in the far corner, she discovered a medicine bottle, a small jar of ointment, a piece of cloth and a wad of cotton-wool. Monica picked them up. Usually when Bob was out of sorts, he would soon enough complain. He had never so much as cut his finger while slicing a loaf without coming to her, all fuss, to bandage it. There was something child-like and endearing about him in that respect. It was so strange that he had been taking medicine without telling her. That too was her fault; he had had no chance these last few months. She examined the bottle and the jar. There was no chemist's name on them. On the jar she read the words: *Poison. To be used according to directions.* The name, Mr MacEwan, and the date, were on the bottle. She thought for a moment and saw that the date was only two days earlier, — the day Bob had disappointed her by failing to keep his promise and coming home late. So he had not been working, but seeing the doctor. He was even now, this very day, under doctor's orders. Not their own doctor, either: Monica was familiar with his handwriting. She was assailed by doubt and suspicion. She was now in the grip of foreboding which made the blood race in her head. She put the drawer on the bed and searched under the tissue-paper lining. She found what she was looking for, an official leaflet: *Advice for those suffering from venereal diseases.* She sat down on the bed to read it. Her heart pounded like a great unruly pendulum against her breast. The letters danced before her eyes, mocking every attempt to read and make sense of them.

But one fact stood out straight and clear as a street before her: Bob had been deceiving her. While she had been worrying about not being able to let go of him, he had been rejoicing like a widower in his new-found freedom. How he must have laughed to himself at what she had said in the cemetery and her attempt to open up a space, one of sexual abstinence, between them by talking about her own death, — and he, long since regarding her as a corpse that could not be touched except with kind, unlustful hands. That was what explained his patience with her and his gentleness towards her; his appetite was being sated at some other feast. It was the pity of contempt and indifference, the kind that she had once shown her mother.

Nor had Bob waited, like Ned Rosser, until she had her baby in her arms. In vain had she insisted on keeping other women out of the house. Bob had been wicked in his glee, foiling all her plans, first of all to keep him faithful and then to wean herself from having to care for him. He had doubtless been sleeping with a woman on the night she thought he had left her. That was probably the night he had picked up his infection. Then, having fallen ill, he had realized the danger he was in, planned a way of getting her out of his way, seized the opportunity which she had provided for calling the doctor, and agreed with him in advance to put her in a hospital in town. Thus he had arranged that she would not discover his condition, and thought that, conveniently, she would die in her ignorance.

But the worst nightmare, the one which made the shapeless Monica wince and shudder on the bed, was the thought that her husband that night had risen from the arms of an infected whore, disengaged his body from the deadly contagious coupling, and brought it home, the seeds of corruption having taken root in him and already starting to do their leprous work, to throw himself thus into her arms and against her body. As she thought of their embraces that night Monica tasted blood in her mouth. She had bitten through her lip.

She went into her own bedroom and began to dress. Already her resolution had taken hold and was directing her actions, though she scarcely yet understood the purpose of what she was doing. Her intention had now lodged in her consciousness, and had cast out of it everything that had been strident there a few minutes earlier. It was only sixty minutes since the sound of the doctor's car had faded in her ears and her life had been turned upside down so that nothing was of any importance to her any more except the terrifying knowledge that her life had shrunk to less than a day and that her last moments were drawing near. Now, a mere hour later, only for having found a bottle, a jar and a leaflet in a drawer, the length of her life had been infinitely extended, death had withdrawn beyond the horizon, and the only thing that meant anything to her was her wounded, jealous pride which, as she let down her petticoat over her head and pulled it carefully over her hips, was making her say over and over again, 'I must have proof, I must have proof'.

After all, a medicine bottle and a jar of ointment would not be enough in a court of law. To get a divorce from Bob she would have to obtain evidence of his infidelity and prove beyond all doubt the nature of his disease. The only way she could do that, thought Monica, was by contacting his doctor, and getting him to be a witness. She pulled her stockings up over her knees and secured them loosely with safety-pins, since she could no longer bear garters around her legs. Without thinking of what she was about, she did everything possible as she got dressed to spare her body discomfort. She took a pair of scissors and cut through the stitches of her flat shoes, at the backs above the heel, so that she could slip her feet into them more easily; but all the while her mind was counting how many doctors' surgeries there were in Swansea's Wood Street, where most of the town's practitioners lived. She would have to go from one to the other, and enquire at every house with a brass plaque on it whether that was where her husband had come for treatment. Suddenly she remembered that Bob had warned her, before setting out that morning, that he would be working until seven o'clock. Did not that mean he had an appointment with his doctor after work? Monica looked at her watch: it was already gone five. She could catch the half-past-five bus, and be in town by six. Supposing it would take her ten minutes to walk from the bus-stop to the end of Wood Street, she wondered whether she would be in time to come face-to-face with Bob at the surgery door. That would be perfect revenge. Monica imagined a change coming over his face, his eyes behind his glasses (for Bob had recently become short-sighted) registering first of all his confusion, his refusal to believe it was her, then his disbelief turning into horrified certainty. No, she would not reproach him, only ask him to hail a taxi to take them home; and then, in the car and in the house, she would make him confess, she would get all the facts out of him; she would get from him the name of his doctor, and get a description of the woman and the house where they had been together, she would learn how he had met her; she would raise his hopes too and loosen his tongue by telling him: 'I won't forgive you unless you tell me the story in full, the whole truth'. In this way, by threats and promises, she would get the story out of him. Monica discovered that her curiosity, her wish to know, was just as intense as her craving for revenge.

The thought that there was another Bob besides the Bob she knew, a Bob who could be brought to life by the looks and behaviour of another woman who provided him with experiences unknown to her; the thought, too, that another woman living miles away could by chance describe a man who had once slept with her, describe his ardour and his laugh and his way of making love, and this man perhaps completely different from the one who had shared her bed for years, so that in listening to the unknown woman's words she would not imagine that they were the same man; this thought of an unknown Bob stimulated Monica's curiosity. She had never before considered that curiosity could be such a strong part of jealousy. He has another life that I know nothing about, she told herself. He came into my bed that night without my suspecting for a moment that he'd just left the arms of another woman, and a filthy prostitute at that. What sort of a man is he, after all? What do I know about him? Well, she would insist on knowing, she was going to get Bob himself to satisfy her. Her Bob would drag up the other Bob before her eyes, the one she did not know, and reveal him to her in all his nakedness on an unfamiliar bed. By minutely questioning — she would spare him nothing, not even the most intimate details — she would insist on laying bare everything he had done that night. She knew full well how to cross-examine him, how to play on him to good effect. And then, having got it all out of him, having defiled him in the mire of what he remembered, she would cast him from her, and send the facts to her father's old solicitor in Cardiff, and Bob would know the full force of her revenge. She was not one to forgive like Mrs Rosser. She finished dressing. She slammed the front door behind her.

Miss Evans tapped on her window and waved in greeting, but Monica did not look up. Mrs North ran to her front door, lifted the flap of the letter-box and peered through it. She called out to her daughter:

'Good heavens, Mrs MacEwan's going into the village. Do you see her?'

'How can I while you're looking out?'

'She's sailing along like a ship in a storm. What did the doctor say to her, I wonder? She looks ghastly, as though she's been drinking. See how unsteadily she's walking. Where will she go? I'd give a whole bottle of brandy to know. Run to the post-office, my girl, and buy a halfpenny stamp and see whether she's taking the bus.'

At the end of the road Mrs Clarence and the curate were chatting about the annual outing of the Mothers' Union. They saw Monica approaching. The curate doubled up in a fit of coughing. Mrs Clarence stuck her nose in the air like a church steeple pointing heavenwards. When Mrs Valmai Briand saw Monica, as she plucked her eyebrows at a mirror in her bedroom window, she flopped onto her bed with laughter. Thus did Church Road bid farewell to Monica MacEwan.

The bus was ten minutes late and Monica had to wait for it at the end of the road. It was a sunny, sultry afternoon; the women passing by in their summer frocks looked at her in astonishment as she stood there in a long coat which failed to conceal her swollen body. Monica could feel the hot flushes around her womb, she wiped away perspiration from her neck and face, and already her shoes were pinching her feet. She was glad to sink into her seat on the bus. She tried to keep her mind from wandering from her errand: I must stick it out to the end, she told herself. But the bus jolted her so painfully that she had to hold onto the seat in front with both hands. Every sudden stop to pick up passengers, every restart and change of gear, shook and hurt her. The bus filled up as it came into town, but there was just enough room for one little boy on the seat next to Monica. She pushed her hat back off her forehead and undid her coat to cool her chest, and the child peeked up at her flushed face. His mother prodded him in the back, whispering, 'Don't stare,' but Monica had closed her eyes and heard nothing. She was aware only of her pain and her mission. Already her contractions were becoming more frequent, like a flood-tide, and threatening to weaken her resolve. She began to wish she was at home, she did not have the strength, she had been too reckless. But soon she heard the voice of the bus-conductor shouting: 'Terminus!'

The bus had stopped near the market. Wood Street was a thoroughfare leading from the town's western side to the prosperous suburbs on the outskirts of Gower. Monica made in that direction. It was the shops' closing-time: all around her there were cars and pedestrians making their way home; the noisy trams were clattering past, the cars' horns were blaring, shop-girls and young executives were running to catch bus or train. Swansea, with its uncivic, bustling streets, seemed a huge ants' nest that had been roughly turned over by a spade. For Monica, though brought up in a city, there was something shabby about the bustle and the rows of unlovely shops that made her steel herself as she proceeded on her vengeful way. No, I shall not forgive him, she thought, he has to pay for his filthy tricks, the dirty dog. What infuriated her in these streets was his baseness, the vile lowness of his character. She felt a desire to grind her heel in his face. She quickened her pace as much as she could. By the time she had reached the end of Wood Street she was out of breath. She stopped, leaning against a telephone kiosk at the corner.

The scene had changed. In front of her there was a wide, well-kept road with two rows of leafy trees, like a boulevard, on either side of her. The houses behind them had been built in the nineteenth century. They had none of the elegance of town streets of the eighteenth century, but they were tall with four storeys to each. They stood in rows of about the same height, quiet and dignified, proclaiming that behind their heavy doors and the stone of their bay-windows there was an orderly, leisurely family life and a tradition of grace and stability.

It was at these solid doors she meant to knock. In those spacious rooms she would have to explain the nature of her loathsome mission. It was not as easy as she had supposed to search for shameful evidence here. There was a reserved, discreet look about the houses. They seemed to say to all who passed by that human life was too precious to be trampled underfoot and had a right to be respected and cherished. Monica could already hear them rebuking her for her enquiry.

She hesitated and felt down at heart, and again she became aware of her contractions. She would have to hurry, or her strength would fail her. She gritted her teeth and moved on. She came to the first brass plate, opened the iron gate and rang the bell.

She knew no more until she was sitting on a deep sofa and a tall, middle-aged man was standing before her. She had not noticed that she had been waiting some ten minutes in this large room, which was even more spacious than she had expected, with one of Frank Brangwyn's engravings on the wall opposite. She revived from her half-swoon on hearing a voice above her asking:

'Well, Madam?'

She answered in wild haste:

'I want to know about my husband. Are you his doctor? I must know the nature of his disease. As a matter of fact, I do know,' and she handed the leaflet to the doctor. 'But I must have your say-so to prove it. I can't get divorced from him without it, and I must —'

'Excuse me for interrupting you. May I have your name and the name of your husband?'

'MacEwan, Robert MacEwan. He's a fairly slim man, with dark hair and spectacles —'

'There's no one of that name among my patients. Who sent you here?'

'No one. I came here first because I'm going to search —'

'Just a minute, Mrs MacEwan. Now, listen to me —'

But Monica did not listen. It was enough for her to know that Bob was not here. She longed to escape, to move on to the next doctor. She was in a hurry. She heard the voice going on in the kind, worldly-wise tone that is often adopted by doctors. He was rambling on about the rights of patients to confidentiality and the responsibility and ethical practices of the medical profession. Monica thought it was the street talking to her, the voice and words were so like what she had been expecting. She tried to rise from the sofa, but flopped back onto it. The doctor fell silent and looked at her intently.

'Stay here quietly,' he said in an authoritative voice.

He went out and returned immediately with a tumbler.

'Drink this,' he said, 'and keep still. I'll be back in two minutes.'

The doctor went out to telephone and rang the nearest surgery, about fifty yards farther up Wood Street:

'Is that you, R —?'

'Yes.'

'A word of warning. I've an awful woman here who's going around asking who her husband's doctor is. The man's name is MacEwan, and he has something venereal, I should think. Anyway, his wife's out for his blood. I thought I should warn you, before I see her out. Will you pass the word along?'

The voice at the other end of the line laughed:

'All right, thank you. MacEwan's in my clinic at this very moment and he has a terrific dose. I'll make sure she doesn't see him.'

The doctor went back in to Monica:

'Are you feeling better?'

'Yes, thank you.'

She got to her feet.

'Now then, Mrs MacEwan, the best thing for you is to take a taxi straight home. If you don't, you'll do yourself a lot of harm. Just consider: what if you went into labour in the street? Please bear in mind that the fact your husband has a disease is no proof that he's been unfaithful. There are more ways than one of catching a disease. And even if he has, he's already been punished enough. You have sufficient cause for concern about yourself without looking for trouble. Good-day to you.'

She found herself in the street again, moving on to the next brass plate. But the doctor's words had made her see things in a different light: why was she bothering if a doctor's evidence would not be sufficient in a divorce court? The mental picture of Bob in bed with a woman of the streets began to lose some of its clarity. She felt her hatred for him beginning to subside, and a tired apathy obliterating it. Her mind began to wander. She remembered her horror of prostitutes and their clients from her days as a girl in Cardiff, a horror which she had never understood, but which had remained a vital part of the memories of her nightly wanderings. Perhaps it was horror at one of the bogeys of her adolescence which, despite her pain and discomfort, had been driving her on this futile errand. She was the same person now as she had been all those years ago in the streets of Cardiff. Nor would she ever be different. She had lived long enough to know that character is formed by what we make of our early years. That is what is so cruel about our fate: it is what takes shape inside us during the least self-conscious period of our lives, when neither reason nor judgement exercises control over our blood, which rules us right up to our dying breath. Monica recalled the idols of her youth, Cleopatra and Pompadour: what had they been if not whores? Perhaps the horror she felt of street-women was nothing but a fear of looking too closely at her own ideal. Listless and indifferent now, she said: 'Perhaps that's what I am too.'

She looked up. Doctor R—'s surgery was close by. But what did she want there? Now at last her quest seemed strange and inexplicable. Scarcely could she take it in that she had gone to the trouble of coming here from Newton to seek revenge on one in whom she had lost all interest. Bob could go free. Was it really he who had brought her here? Suddenly she understood and remembered: she had not intended to persecute Bob at all, only to escape from the loneliness of that house where she had been given a death-sentence, to escape from the horrible threat, to put a veil between her and tomorrow by keeping busy, to fill her mind, to rack her limbs, anything and everything to forget. Her hand was on Dr R—'s gate but she let go of it. She slumped slowly to the ground.

About three minutes later the doctor opened the door:

'Come back on Monday afternoon, Mr MacEwan, and I'll give you another injection. There's no need to be alarmed, you'll soon be back in perfect health. Good heavens, what's that woman doing lying on the pavement? Hey, help, help . . . .'

Afterword

Though little known outside Wales, John Saunders Lewis (1893-1985) has been one of the most significant and controversial figures in Welsh life during this century. In Welsh literature, he is the foremost dramatist, and a poet whose poems, though few, are of the highest quality. As the most important critic and historian of Welsh and European literatures, he displayed the immense intellect of a widely-read scholar. In particular, his researches revealed and interpreted the rich literary heritage of medieval Catholic Wales, and brought about an important change in the way of viewing Wales's literary tradition. He was one of the founders of the Welsh Nationalist Party, and for many years its president and editor of its paper; for the cause, he was a diligent pamphleteer, and for the cause he went to prison and sacrificed his academic and artistic career. Having failed as politician, he latterly returned to his first love, the theatre, and established himself as a major dramatist.

Little in his early life suggested his subsequent career. He was born in England, in Wallasey, the son of a cultured Welsh Presbyterian minister. At the turn of the century the Liverpool Welsh community was huge (perhaps about 100,000) and one might spend one's life in it and seldom have to speak English. The Welsh cultural and religious life was vigorous: Liverpool was to all intents and purposes the capital of North Wales. Nevertheless, from his Welsh-speaking home, Saunders Lewis was sent to a private school, Liscard High School for Boys, where he imbibed gratefully all the 'public school' values — love of England, and of English literature, reverence for aristocracy and monarchy, admiration for the British military tradition. As he later admitted, at that time Wales and Welsh meant nothing to him; he loved the theatre, and English and Anglo-Irish poetry and theatre; he dreamed of being an English man of letters. In 1911 he went to Liverpool University to study for a degree in English, and there met his future wife, Margaret Gilcriest, of an Irish Protestant family, and romantically attached to the Fenian cause. His studies were interrupted by the outbreak of war: he volunteered, and served as second lieutenant in the South Wales Borderers in France and was wounded in action.

While on service his readings of the novels of Maurice Barrès had convinced him that a creative artist needed to return to his cultural roots, and he became a (cultural) nationalist, resolved on a career as a writer using the myths and legends of Wales, doing for Wales what Yeats, Synge and the Anglo-Irish had done for Ireland, but in English, not Welsh. He returned to the University and gained a first-class degree in English, and began research on the influence of the English 'Augustan' writers on Welsh literature. His father had retired to Swansea, and Saunders Lewis determined to settle in Wales to pursue his new vision.

In 1922 he was appointed lecturer in Welsh literature at the newly-formed University College of Swansea. His letters reveal a profound dislike of almost everything about Wales ('I hate Wales', he writes at one point) — its joyless and austerely puritan religiosity, its amateurish theatre, its deplorable critical standards in literature, its prevailing Liberal/Labour political mindset, its provinciality, its grovelling subservience to everything English, its disregard of its own language and ignorance of its own rich literary heritage. In 1924 he married Margaret Gilcriest, who had been converted to Catholicism. In 1925, convinced that only by political action could Wales survive, he and others founded the Welsh Nationalist Party, pledged to seek autonomy for Wales under the Crown, to secure the economic well-being of Wales and restore Welsh as the first language of the nation. He soon became its president (1926-1939) and editor of its paper, *Y Ddraig Goch*.

In 1932 he was received into the Catholic Church and offered to resign as President of the Party: anti-Catholic feeling in Wales was still a force to be reckoned with by a tiny political party. By 1936 the Party had made no progress whatsoever. Fifteen years earlier, Saunders Lewis had said: 'It would be a great blessing for Wales if some Welshman did something for his nation that caused him to be put in prison'. A *cause célèbre* was needed. At last came a pretext. The English Government had ridden roughshod over widespread protests in Wales, to build a bombing school at Penyberth, in the Llŷn Peninsula, in the heart of Welsh-speaking Wales, a country that affected to be profoundly pacifist. One night Saunders Lewis and two other patriots committed arson on the building site, as a symbolic gesture, and surrendered to the police.

At their trial in Caernarfon, Saunders Lewis was not allowed to plead in Welsh, but went on to proclaim that the moral law, the laws of God, ranked higher than those of the English Government. The jury could not agree on a verdict and the case was transferred to the Old Bailey where the three were found guilty without further ado and sent to Wormwood Scrubs for nine months. On leaving prison he found that he had lost his post at Swansea; he, his wife and daughter were almost destitute. Though the three were welcomed in large and enthusiastic rallies, the token act of rebellion did not lead to the Nationalist cause sweeping Wales: by then, a war in Europe was clearly imminent, and the arson in fact looked perilously like high treason. Saunders Lewis was almost universally reviled and blacklisted from holding any academic post. He spent the years from 1937 to 1952 at Llanfarian near Aberystwyth, eking out a meagre living on a smallholding with some teaching and journalism. His weekly column 'Cwrs y Byd' ('The Way of the World') in the weekly paper *Baner ac Amserau Cymru* is regarded as a monument of journalism: in it he commented on current affairs and the course of the war, on European and world politics, on domestic issues affecting Wales, and reviewed new books. In 1943 he stood as a candidate in the election of the MP for the University of Wales, but was beaten by his opponent Prof W.J. Gruffydd, an erstwhile friend and nationalist.

In 1947 his interest in the theatre revived. His old friends, the Catholic Wynne family of Garthewin Hall in Denbighshire had set up a little theatre where an annual festival was held. This encouraged Saunders Lewis to write plays for the festival, and later for Welsh radio and television. In 1952 Saunders Lewis was appointed Lecturer in Welsh at the University College, Cardiff, and moved to Penarth. He retired in 1957. In 1962 he delivered a radio talk on 'Tynged yr Iaith' ('The Fate of the Language'), in which he forecast the extinction of the Welsh language unless a political campaign were begun — entailing civil disobedience, infringements of the law, protests and perhaps imprisonment. Independence was worthless without our language, our most distinctive badge. As a result there was created Cymdeithas yr Iaith Gymraeg (the Welsh Language Society) which began a vigorous and still continuing campaign for the rights of Welsh-speakers, making the topic a political issue. He became its Honorary President in 1963 but eventually resigned when the Society (imagining it was following Saunders Lewis's own example in 1936) manifested a certain hostility to the rocket-testing range at Aberporth. By now Saunders Lewis, mindful of his days in the army, to which he looked back with pride, argued that every country has a right to defend itself. Though, back in 1936, he had been an admirer of the Prince of Wales (later Edward VIII), by 1969 he was hostile to the Investiture of Prince Charles as Prince of Wales, regarding it as a Labour Government stunt foisted on the Royal Family to try to thwart Welsh Nationalism. He was one of the rare Nationalists to speak up for the 'naïve and romantic soldiers' of the so-called Free Wales Army who were gaoled in that year. They, after all, had come nearest to the 'citizens' army' whose formation he had advocated back in 1923.

Letters written by Saunders Lewis to his old friend Robert Wynne confirm the impression given by his final plays and poems — that he was bitter and totally disillusioned after a lifetime and a career sacrificed in vain for an ungrateful Wales: though still sustained by his Catholic faith, old age and infirmity made him yearn for death. The University of Wales awarded him an honorary Doctorate in 1983. Mrs Lewis died in 1984 and Dr Lewis in 1985. At his funeral it was revealed that in 1975 Pope Paul VI had made Saunders Lewis a Knight Commander of the Order of Saint Gregory — one of the highest honours open to a Catholic layman.

As a creative writer, Saunders Lewis distinguished himself as a dramatist and, to a lesser extent, a poet. Apart from some juvenilia in his school's magazine, his earliest creative work is seen in the English poems, pastiches of the Georgian and especially Anglo-Irish poets, addressed to his sweetheart in letters to her, and only recently published. His first published creative work was a little comedy in English, *The Eve of Saint John* (1921), inspired mainly by Synge's *The Shadow of the Glen*. It was written in a poetic Anglo-Welsh of the author's own devising, quite unlike any real-life Anglo-Welsh — which he abhorred. By his own admission, he was not satisfied with the diction he had invented, and felt he had to turn to Welsh as his artistic medium. Accordingly, in 1922, he published *Gwaed yr Uchelwyr*, a three-act tragedy set in rural Wales in 1827 (translated as *Noble Blood* by J.P. Clancy). The somewhat stilted style and unhappy ending in this story of a heroine who, because of the dictates of honour refused to marry her true love, even though she could thereby save her family from enforced exile, meant that the play was not well received. In 1924 he published *Doctor er ei Waethaf*, a stilted and bowdler-ized version of Molière's *Le Médecin malgré lui* which, despite its defects, is still occasionally staged. In 1923 and 1925, hoping to realize his aim of doing for Welsh legend what Yeats and Lady Gregory had done for Irish legends, he published the first two acts of a verse tragedy, *Blodeuwedd*, based on one of the tales in the medieval Four Branches of the Mabinogi. Pressure of work for the Nationalist cause meant that the play was not to be completed till 1948.

Thus in 1930, after three largely abortive experiments in the theatre, Saunders Lewis was far better known as a literary historian and critic endowed with a powerful intellect and original, often controversial, views on the Welsh literary tradition: witness his *A School of Welsh Augustans* (1924), his *Williams Pantycelyn* (1927), a study of Wales's greatest religious poet; and his *Ceiriog* (1929), a sympathetic and intuitive study of a Victorian lyricist whom he regarded as 'an artist in Philistia'.

Monica was thus a new departure for its author, and was to be little better received than his plays. He seems, in part, to have written *Monica* as a challenge to Welsh novelists to do better. In his pamphlet *An Introduction to Contemporary Welsh Literature* (1926) he had been very scathing about both Welsh drama and novels. Of the only novel he thought worthy of notice, Tegla Davies's *Gŵr Pen y Bryn* (*The Master of Pen y Bryn*), he says it is 'the one serious attempt at a full-sized

96

psychological novel . . . unhappily . . . what should have been a rigorous study in the development of a weak nature turns in the end to piety and edification . . . . He [sc. the author] wants to save people, even the people of imagination. He cannot leave them to complete the evil that is in them, but must convert them to repentance and amiability'.

Elsewhere, in his 'Llythyr ynghylch Catholigiaeth' ('Letter concerning Catholicism') published in the periodical *Y Llenor* (1926), he had castigated those authors who had 'lost the sense of sin in literature . . . sin is the substance of the classical novels'.

The literary influences on the choice of subject matter are not hard to find. *Monica* is provokingly dedicated to William Williams of Pantycelyn, 'onelie begetter of this mode of writing', a reference not to Williams's hymns but to his less well-known *Ductor Nuptiarum neu Gyfarwyddwr Priodas* (*Ductor Nuptiarum or Guide to Marriage*), of which Saunders Lewis has said, 'In it we get for the first time in literature not only a portrayal but also a critical analysis and definition of romantic love'. In the form of three dialogues, it relates the story of Martha Pseudogam, a lapsed believer whose unhappy marriage has been based solely on carnal desires, on 'romantic love', rather than entered into for the purpose of raising a family and creating a home, thereby making of life a communion. Both Williams and Saunders Lewis recognized the power of 'romantic love' and condemned it as an absolutely dangerous and self-destructive antisocial force.

He found closer literary models in French literature. The novel has been compared to Gustave Flaubert's *Madame Bovary* (1857). Each author, while seemingly objective, betrays a discreet sympathy for his hapless heroine. In both novels, the heroine's social world is satirized. Just as Emma Bovary dreams of being one of the great courtesans and adulteresses of history of whom she has read, so Monica sees herself as an oriental priestess sacrificing her husband, and thinks of herself as resembling Cleopatra, Pompeia, Pompadour. In each case there is a seemingly inevitable downward slide from naïvely romantic imaginings to the sordid and ultimately unsatisfying reality of sex.

A more immediate model, as Saunders Lewis admitted to me, was François Mauriac's *Thérèse Desqueyroux* (1927), with its lonely, tormented, agnostic heroine who tries to poison her insensitive husband, is acquitted for lack of evidence, and returns to ostracism by her husband's family. She retires to her bedroom to smoke endless cigarettes and become a slattern. We sense Mauriac's sympathy for his wicked and hapless heroine, who tries to acquire faith by going to church, but to no avail; she is not redeemed at the end, as the author allows his characters to consummate the evil in them and leaves them free to go to damnation.

Saunders Lewis very kindly confirmed to me, in a letter, the influence of Mauriac. However, he revealed that the story, however far-fetched it might have seemed, was based on a real-life case known to him personally:

> She lived next door but one to us in Newton, a village near Mumbles. She died in hospital, not in the street. After her death we saw her father walking her front garden like a man crazed. He had never been there before while she was alive. I was then told by her neighbour how she had snatched her husband from her sister, and told of her suffering during her pregnancy and her staying in bed and the filth. There was very little that was imaginary in the novel, and all the other characters were our neighbours with their names changed slightly, such as Mrs North for Mrs West. I never thought then that one of them might bring a libel action against me since none of them spoke Welsh or read a book. I was dreadfully sorry for the wretched young wife; I called her Monica because St Augustine's mother was a well-known saint, and a saint is one who finally renounces all earthly love; and the theme

of the novel, is showing how my Monica developed through the ghastly purgatory of her last year till she renounced her only treasure, her husband whom she had snatched. I was greatly disappointed when the work was published, that the defenders of the novel believed that the work aimed to teach a moral lesson. I preferred the critics who frowned on its indecency and lack of taste. My interest was in the purgatory of the uneducated young woman, its meaning and effect on her, and the name suggests her end. At that time I did consider a series of novels on others of my neighbours in the same street, but politics and the Party brought me too much work.

(Private letter, September 23, 1977) [My translation]

Nevertheless, even after retiring from political life, Saunders Lewis was to turn to the theatre, and was not to publish another novel until 1964, when he published his little master-piece, *Merch Gwern Hywel* (*The Daughter of Gwern Hywel*), a very different, really romantic novel, again based on a real-life episode, this time in Saunders Lewis's own family.

At first sight *Monica* must seem utterly isolated from the rest of Saunders Lewis's work. Most of his plays are set anywhere but in contemporary Wales. None of them deal with English-speaking, rootless characters from the cities of the industrialized South. Yet a closer examination reveals links. Like Monica, the heroines of *Blodeuwedd* and *Siwan* are passionate, sensual women, unhappy in marriage. When Monica tells Bob she is pregnant, his reply, '"From now on we'll have something to live for" . . . had gone though his wife's mind like a knife . . . She . . . understood that the monotony of love-making, and a surfeit of it, had taken root in him also.' Similarly in *Blodeuwedd*, Act II, the heroine entreats her husband:

	Ah God, my Llew, if once you would look at me
	And say, 'You, you are my fulfilment'.
	If you would say that . . .
Llew:	I will say it when your son is on your arm.
Blodeuwedd:	A word like fate . . .

Llew's tactless, unthinking reply to his childless wife seals his fate: with her lover she plots to kill him. No woman with self-respect likes to be thought of as worthy of love only if she satisfies her husband's desire for an heir. So Monica, too, resolves to punish Bob, even if it entails the death of her unborn child. Recent critics have scented patriarchism here and elsewhere, in that much space is given to depicting Bob as a decent enough chap, wronged by his irrational wife. However, the picture of Bob is not a flattering one: he wallows in self-pity and should have shown more firmness as well as tenderness towards his wife. Bob is, like Llew in *Blodeuwedd*, a weak and obtuse character, who cannot understand his wife, and indeed he is the forerunner of a good many other inept men, linked to more resolute women, in Saunders Lewis's theatre.

In Chapter Five, it seems out of character that the ignorant, ill-educated heroine should be able to explain herself at such length, and so lucidly, to her husband, and, after the doctor has left her, that her thoughts should be so profound and so artistically expressed. The author himself draws attention to this inconsistency: 'she had relished her melodramatic speech in the cemetery and enjoyed her husband's obvious embarrassment and the clarity of her own vision and the trenchancy of her own words'. However, in these passages, there are eerie foreshadowings of themes which were to emerge again in the author's final plays, where a keen note of disillusion is often heard. Monica has no faith to sustain her, no sense of purpose in life: after the doctor's diagnosis she accepts, even welcomes, death: 'She had even taken her leave of lying. By what discipline had she learned at last to deny herself the vacuous fantasies that had been a veil between her and the *nothingness of existence*?' [my italics]. This existentialist sentiment was to be echoed much later, in *Serch yw'r Doctor* (*Love's the Doctor*)(1958) where the chorus of cynical villagers is given the line 'Let's pretend there's a purpose to life,' striking an odd note in this pastiche of a Molière comedy. Monica's meditations on her coming death, in which she likens herself to a condemned prisoner consoling himself as he awaits the result of his appeal for a reprieve, uncannily anticipate the thoughts of the panic-stricken Meursault in the condemned cell in Camus' *L'Etranger* (1942), and foreshadow Saunders Lewis's own grim playlet, *Cell y Grog* (*The Condemned Cell*) (1975), in which it is clear that prison is a hell on earth, an allegory of the human condition and in particular of the author's own existence, as, aged and infirm, after a life of failure and disappointment, he dragged out his life: The Prisoner says, 'I've lived thirty years and it was all folly. There's no meaning in death either'. The Officer too dreads his future: 'Prison is . . . Hell between grey walls. And everyone . . . is sick and tired of the filthy, hopeless, pointless existence . . . . Death makes everyone better off,' welcoming death, as Monica had done. In 1930, the author had been a practising believer, a secret Catholic, who could pity his wretched heroine as, doomed by her lack of any belief, she slid inevitably into oblivion: his own faith assured him that death was not the end, that there was a purpose in existence. By the end, however, he had come to express sentiments that echo those of Monica most poignantly. Indeed I think *Monica* must be among the earliest existentialist novels, if not the earliest.

During Monica's morbid visit to the cemetery, she and Bob remind each other of what they had witnessed there on Palm Sunday: 'Rich and poor . . . were to be seen side by side arranging flowers and trimming the grass. This is an old custom which had survived all the revolutions of South Wales and although there is scarcely anyone on Palm Sunday afternoon who whispers the *memento etiam Domine* now, yet the hands move tenderly and reverently at their task, as if they at least remember and implore'. Here the author only hints at a message he had spelt out a little earlier in his 'Myfyrdod Sul y Blodau' ('Meditation on Palm Sunday') (in *Y Ddraig Goch*,

April 1929) where he pictures relatives decking their family graves, and muses:

> We are all one family here, the needy toil next to the well-to-do. For the dead unite us one with another. The transient characteristics, the fortuitous differences, the consciousness of superficial things, disappear. Today the Welsh are at the cemetery, in the company of their fore-fathers. Wales hearkens to the speech of the past, and we know that we are one. It is the dead, the past, that unites us. It is the future, the uncertainty, that divides us. Yet that dividing too will be an enrichment if we continue every Palm Sunday and oftener to commune with the past, . . . Isn't that why I am a member of the National Party?

However, in the novel, the significance of this custom, and the comfort it brings, are clearly quite lost on Bob and Monica, cut off as they are from all Welsh traditions and beliefs. As one critic remarked, they might as well be living in Harrogate, and the novel could be seen as a warning, that one day soon, all Wales's citizens will live rootless, purposeless lives in decent, godless and snobbish petty bourgeois suburbs.

The critical reception afforded *Monica* ranged from the lukewarm to the utterly hostile. It was savaged by Iorwerth C. Peate in *Y Tyst* (February 12, 1931). He attacked not only the novelist's craftsmanship but also his subject-matter:

> One of the defects of this story is that the author clearly suffers from a complex, and sees only what his complex permits. The author would have done better to pay more attention to biology and less to the foolish modern psychology taught by people who talk of sex knowing next to nothing about its basics. Had he done so, he would not have written this shallow story . . . . It leaves a foul taste in one's mouth, and it is long since anything was published in Welsh which left one reader at least so sad about the future of our country's literature.

In *Y Llenor* (Spring 1931), J.H. Morgan was favourable but

apologetic: 'However much this novel and its author may be blamed and scorned — and the author will suffer more than his work, until the Welsh critical tradition has more dignity — let us try to bear in mind that the author, as a Welsh artist, has a perfect right to deal with natural acts and their consequences'. The editor, W.J. Gruffydd, was equally sympathetic. Thomas Parry, in *Yr Efrydydd* (March, 1931), was more forthright: 'The author narrates his story equably, without losing his temper with anyone or taking offence at anything. We hear no sermon to the effect that afflictions follow sin, the fact is simply expressed that that is what happened here. An example of the self-control of the true artist.'

By and large, critics appear to have been offended by the admission, unheard of in Welsh novels, that the physical side of marriage existed; the unedifying spectacle of Monica's lust, the sleazy details of her lying in her own filth, Bob's night with a prostitute, his V.D., the prospect of an abortion — all these were bad enough, and alien to the tradition of the Welsh novel. Even worse was the author's apparently objective attitude, not condemning what he described, refusing to moralize, refusing to supply some happy ending in which Monica would repent and somehow be saved. Though the author meant to preach no moral lesson, in retrospect the novel seems moral enough: Monica is punished by her own despair and dies, and Bob, for one night's infidelity, catches V.D. What could be more moral?

The novel has never been popular; the reception was discouraging, and Saunders Lewis was clearly more at ease writing dramatic dialogue than narrative prose. No other Welsh novelist was to follow where he had ventured. Ironically, had the novel been published in English, the language of the characters in the novel, it would not have aroused such hostility and might have been welcomed as a significant contribution to Anglo-Welsh literature. To readers of Welsh-language novels, *Monica* depicted an utterly alien world. In recent years, however, critics have rediscovered the novel and begun to analyse it with greater sympathy. Writing in 1975, the novelist Islwyn Ffowc Elis concluded a penetrating analysis thus: 'Despite its failings . . . I would set it safely in the "top ten" of Welsh novels by virtue of its skilful structure, its rich thought, its penetrating portrayals and social observation, and the spell cast by Saunders Lewis's prose style' (In *Saunders Lewis*, ed. D.T. Lloyd and G.R. Hughes, 1975). Likewise Delyth Ann George, writing in *Y Traethodydd* (vol. CXLI, 1986), while noting shortcomings in *Monica*, such as the alleged patriarchism of the author and some melodramatic touches, concludes: 'Despite the defects noted, *Monica* stands as a memorable milestone in the history of the Welsh novel. At last its doors were opened to a world of psychology that had been firmly shut by the nonconformist puritanism of the last century'. Those for whom the Welsh text was a closed book, may now, in this, Meic Stephens's careful, polished and sympathetic translation, read Monica's poignant story and judge it for themselves.

Bruce Griffiths
March 1997

A Note on the Text

Saunders Lewis's short novel, *Monica*, was first published by Gwasg Aberystwyth in 1930. It was re-issued in 1989 by Gwasg Gomer. For permission to publish this English translation Seren is grateful to Gwasg Gomer and the Trustees of Saunders Lewis's Estate.

The translator wishes to thank Dr R. Geraint Gruffydd, Professor M. Wynn Thomas, Mr Don Dale-Jones and Mr Sam Adams for reading parts of this translation in draft form, and in particular Dr Bruce Griffiths, author of the monograph on Saunders Lewis in the *Writers of Wales* series, for reading the entire English text and making a number of valuable suggestions.

For any infelicities which may remain the translator alone should be held responsible.

The original Welsh edition of this novel had the following epigraph: 'All the characters in this story are imaginary. The author dedicates the story to the memory of Williams of Pantycelyn, onelie begetter of this mode of writing.'

About the Translator

Meic Stephens teaches courses in Journalism, Modern Fiction and Welsh Writing in English at the University of Glamorgan. He has translated the memoirs of Gwynfor Evans, a selection of essays by twentieth-century Welsh writers and, from the French, a book about the Basques. For Seren he edited *A Cardiff Anthology* and *A Rhondda Anthology*. He is co-editor of the *Writers of Wales* series and *The Oxford Literary Guide to Britain and Ireland*. New editions of his *Companion to the Literature of Wales* are due to appear in 1997 and 1998.

About Bruce Griffiths

Bruce Griffiths lectures in French at the University of Wales, Bangor, where he is a Reader. He has published Welsh translations of Molière, Camus and Bordeaux and was the editor of the Welsh Academy's series of translations of modern novels into Welsh. From 1975-1995 he was the editor of the Academy's *English-Welsh Dictionary* (1995). He has published a monograph on *Saunders Lewis* in the *Writers of Wales* series (1979, reissued 1989) and a lecture: *Y Dieithryn wrth y drws* (1993), and has contributed several articles and reviews on Saunders Lewis.